Pride Publishing books by Angel Martinez:

AURA
Quinn's Gambit
Flax's Pursuit
Kellen's Awakening

Offbeat Crimes
Lime Gelatin and Other Monsters
The Pill Bugs of Time

Anthologies:
50s Mixed Tape: The Line

OFFBEAT CRIMES
Volume One

Lime Gelatin and Other Monsters

The Pill Bugs of Time

ANGEL MARTINEZ

Offbeat Crimes Volume One
ISBN # 978-1-78686-049-1
©Copyright Angel Martinez 2016
Cover Art by Posh Gosh ©Copyright September 2016
Interior text design by Claire Siemaszkiewicz
Pride Publishing

Published in 2016 by Pride Publishing, Newland House, The Point, Weaver Road, Lincoln, LN6 3QN, United Kingdom.

Pride Publishing is a subsidiary of Totally Entwined Group Limited.

LIME GELATIN AND OTHER MONSTERS

Dedication

For my two Michelles. They know why.

Chapter One

Strange how half the briefing room chairs were empty and still there was no place to sit. Kyle surveyed his choices, trying to pick the least of several evils, mindful that he was ten minutes early with greater evils yet to come.

He decided on a chair far to the left, in the row behind Loveless and in front of Zacchini. That way he might have odd cravings or sudden flashes of disconnected images for the next two hours, but he could handle it. Neither of these would harm anyone around him. The precinct didn't have enough officers to fill the room, so no one would *need* to sit near him.

Someone always seemed to forget.

Krisk shambled in, blinked slowly at Kyle with his slit-pupiled golden eyes, and wandered to the other side of the room. No one could explain to him how Krisk had made it through the police academy, or why he had wanted to. The lizard man seemed to understand human speech, though he never spoke, and the legality of his arrests had to be questionable.

Gatling, Lourdes and Wolf all wandered in with early-morning bleary eyes but were aware enough to avoid Kyle's side of the room. Only Lourdes should have been worried, but it was becoming habit for his department colleagues to give him a wide berth.

The steady, military *tick-tick-tick* of Lieutenant Dunfee's heels reached them from the hallway and everyone scrambled to settle, eyes front and at least pretending attention. She patted Kyle's shoulder absently as she stalked by, perhaps reminding him that she, at least, had no need to fear his abilities.

The lieutenant tapped her papers straight on the lectern at the front of the room, her hard gaze pinning her officers one by one. "Good morning, ladies and gentle—"

Running footsteps interrupted her as Officer Virago skidded to a halt in the hallway then changed course to rush into the briefing room.

"Damn it, Vance, if you can't get here on time, don't make such a production out of gracing us with your presence," Lieutenant Dunfee snapped.

Virago shot her an unrepentant grin and plopped down two chairs over from Kyle. Normally, Kyle would have moved or warned him off, but the lieutenant was speaking again. Interrupting her a second time, now that she'd started roll call, didn't feel like the best idea. *I can hold this together. Just a few minutes. Nothing has to happen.*

"Loveless?"

In front of Kyle, Carrington Loveless III raised his marshmallow-white hand languidly. "Here."

See? Nothing's happening. It's fine.

"Monroe?"

Kyle raised his hand in acknowledgment and a gout of flame rocketed from his fingers to slam into the ceiling. He yanked his hand down, tucked both hands under his thighs and cringed amid a rain of burned ceiling tile shreddings and mortification.

"Here," he choked out.

"Vance! Move!" the lieutenant bellowed. "Damn it, you know better!"

Virago scrambled out of his seat and claimed a spot standing along the opposite wall. "It's raining out, ma'am! How'm I supposed to know Kirby can suck up my shit when I can't even get a spark?"

"Watch the language, and what did I tell you about that nickname?"

Virago ducked his head with a muttered apology, but more than one person in Kyle's hearing grumbled that the nickname fit too well.

"Sorry, ma'am."

"Not something you can control, Monroe. But these other chuckleheads can be a little more cognizant of where they are in relation to you."

"Yes, ma'am."

With an exasperated shake of her head, she finished roll call, confirmed assignments, then waved someone unfamiliar up from the front row. "Boys and girls, this is our newest officer, Vikash Soren."

Kyle sat up straighter, shifting to see between the heads in front of him. Soren looked like a poster boy for the model police officer, tall and straight, uniform crisp and sharp. He stood at parade rest beside the lieutenant, impassively surveying his new colleagues. A little knot of resentment lodged in Kyle's stomach. At his own introduction to the 77th, he'd been nervous and fidgety, freaked out by the collection of...freaks. *How can he be so calm?*

"Officer Soren transferred from the Harrisburg PD—"

"Don't they have enough freaky shit of their own up there?" Wolf called out in his rasping growl.

"Since Harrisburg is in our jurisdiction," she continued with a quelling glance, "he'll start out partnered with Monroe."

"What does he do, ma'am? That it's safe to put him with Kirby, er, Kyle?" Shira Lourdes asked as she flicked nervous glances across the room at Kyle. An empty chair slid away from her and fell over. Her partner, Greg Santos, shook his head and righted the unfortunate piece of furniture.

"Officer Soren's abilities are his business, which he may or may not choose to share if you ask. And don't bully him about it either, any of you." Lieutenant Dunfee swept the room again, pinning each of her officers like captive butterflies with her needle-laser gaze. "Monroe, my office after briefing. Info on your current case."

She dismissed them, stalking from the room with thunderclouds in her eyes. Kyle found himself approaching the new guy and trying his best not to be awkward. Did he offer to shake hands? Was it safe? Would the guy flinch like so many people did at the sight of Kyle's scarred hands? Soren was even taller up close, six-foot-three of lean inscrutability, his blue eyes startlingly bright against smoky bronze skin.

"Um, hi, I'm Kyle Monroe." Kyle fidgeted when Soren didn't offer his hand either. "You're with me, I guess. I'll show you our spot in the squad room."

Soren followed him silently and Kyle was starting to wonder if he was like Krisk in the not-speaking department until he finally spoke in a smooth, soft baritone, making Kyle startle and miss a step. "Why do they call you Kirby?"

"You'd hear it sooner or later, I guess." Kyle shrugged. "It's this thing I do, absorbing other people's talents temporarily. If they're close to me. Or touch me. Like Kirby, the little pink dude in the video game."

"Ah."

Just that? Soren didn't edge away, or change expression at all. Was he made of stone? "It's a thing. Everyone here has a thing."

After a few more steps, Soren asked, "Always?"

"What... Oh, was I always like this? Who knows? I mean, maybe I've picked up stray thoughts or something, but no. It's pretty recent. Knowing that I do this."

Kyle took a wide arc around Vance as he entered the squad room, pointing to the double desk in the far corner, well removed from everyone else. "That's ours. Coffee's over there, but you might not want that coffee. Let me grab my file and we'll go see the lieutenant."

A flutter of wings sounded overhead—a brilliant flash of feathers shooting in front of Kyle to land on Carrington's desk at the back of the room. With a raucous call, the pink and neon-blue raven folded his wings and waddled over to snap at Carrington's pen.

"Stop it, Edgar."

"You couldn't get laid at a clusterfuck!" Edgar squawked, making another grab for the pen.

Carrington sighed and handed the ballpoint over. "There. Go play. Try not to get ink all over your feet this time."

Edgar seized the pen in his Pepto-Bismol-colored beak and flew to his perch on the other side of the room where he called out, "Fuck you very much!" then proceeded to draw random lines on the paper tacked up beside his perch for Edgar's art projects.

"So what's your story, Soren?" Vance called across the squad room. "What flies your freak flag?"

"Yeah, what do you do?" Jeff Gatling stopped teleporting his banana from one corner of his desk to the other.

"I don't really do anything," Soren answered as he hefted the empty coffeepot. "Guess I'll make fresh since I'm the new guy."

He opened the top to remove the filter and every human voice in the squad room yelled out, "No!"

Most people would have startled, maybe dropped the carafe. Soren just blinked at the roomful of people gesturing wildly. He took the filter out and emptied it over the trashcan. "Why not?"

"You don't want to do that." Kyle stayed by his desk, a nice safe distance from the coffee station. "That's Larry's job."

"Larry's not keeping up then."

The container of sweetener packets began to rattle. It shivered across the counter and leaped to a messy end, ceramic shards skittering across the floor. The desk that Krisk and Wolf shared rose from the floor several inches then slammed back down. Wolf fled with a squeaking yelp just before the desk flipped on its side.

Soren glanced toward Kyle. "Larry's not a cop, is he?"

"He is...he was! A dead cop. Larry's a ghost. He gets ticked if anyone else makes the coffee. Put the stuff back, please!"

"Larry?" Soren raised his voice but to all appearances remained completely unruffled. "I'm new here. I'm very sorry I invaded your jurisdiction. See? I'm putting the carafe back. Closing the top. Are we good, Larry?"

A breeze ruffled through a stack of papers, but no further mayhem ensued. The carafe slid from its pad on the coffeemaker and floated to the water cooler where

Larry, who never manifested in a visible form, whistled tunelessly while he filled the carafe.

From his dim corner of the room, Carrington said in his dry, genteel way, "Welcome to the Island of Misfit Freaks."

* * * *

Half an hour later, with Soren briefed on the case and instructions to meet Chris Hardin from homicide at the ME's office, Kyle led his new partner down to their assigned squad car. Vikash Soren remained a puzzle, which didn't help Kyle's already jangled nerves.

"I'll drive."

Soren sipped the coffee he'd snagged from a nearby food truck, apparently having reached the conclusion everyone else did with one sip of Larry's coffee. It was on par with wood varnish. "You sure you can reach the pedals?"

Kyle stared at him. If he hadn't seen the man's mouth move, he would've sworn he'd imagined those words. "I am *not* short."

One perfect black eyebrow rose a fraction.

"I'm average. Sure you'll fit in the car?" Kyle shot back, knowing it was childish.

Soren merely smiled without showing his teeth. It wasn't even a pissed-off, tight smile—more like the serene expression on a statue of some ancient, smugly contented god. He folded his long frame into the passenger seat without another word.

I think I hate him. He'd better have some serious flaws, or I'm really going to hate him.

Even his posture sitting in the squad car was perfect. Kyle kept his attention on the Market Street traffic, trying to unclench his jaw.

They'd almost reached the Schuylkill River when Soren, in a voice barely loud enough for conversation, asked, "Island of Misfit Freaks?"

"That's what you've been chewing on all this time?"

"Yes." Soren sipped his coffee, a little V forming between his perfect black eyebrows. "I think I was expecting something…else."

Kyle blew out an explosive breath. Yeah, he got that. "I did, too, when they transferred me. I mean, you hear about other cities, and it's more X-Files, right? And if there's any paranormal cops from Philly with useful talents, they probably get shipped somewhere else. But here, sorry, no. You're stuck with the rejects."

"I understand why you'd be a problem." Soren held up a hand when Kyle sputtered. "Dangerous thing you do, which you can't control, it seems. But the others?"

"Yeah. All of them. Us." Kyle winced at the slip. Four months in this precinct and he still felt like an outsider. "Virago? The one who got chewed out this morning? He's a firestarter."

"All right. But that doesn't sound so odd."

Kyle snickered. "He can only do it when it's dry. Rain, snow, too much humidity, and *poof!* Nothing. Shira Lourdes is a stress telekinetic. Shit flies around when she gets jumpy or upset."

"Hmm. Edgar?"

"We're not sure what his deal is. He came with the lieutenant. My theory is he got caught in some magical crossfire to get the Technicolor feathers. Where the foul mouth, er, beak on him came from is anybody's guess. And Jeff Gatling? Guy with the banana?"

"He does apportation. I could see that."

"Yeah, but he can only teleport fruit."

"Oh." The V-furrow had deepened. Mr. Perfect could be blindsided, apparently.

"That's why they wanted to know what you do. 'Cause seriously? We all do something and we all suck at it."

The Schuylkill, sparkling in the October sunshine, lay behind them before Soren answered. "I don't really *do* anything."

"Then why the hell did they send you to us?" Kyle's voice cracked as his volume rose. He hadn't meant to get snappy, but damn, it was like pulling mastodon teeth using two spoons.

Another sip of coffee, another long silence. "Bad things happen around me."

"Oh, great. That's just great."

"Not all the time." Still Soren managed that soft, even tone, no show of temper, no defensiveness. "Just…when I'm angry."

At the next stoplight, Kyle turned to stare at him. "Soren, do you even *get* angry? Ever?"

"Oh, I do." That smug little smile was back. "You wouldn't like me when I'm angry."

Well, crud. Avengers. Sense of humor. And I was just starting to really hate him. "Ha. Can I call you Bruce?"

"Only if I can call you Tony. Though I'd rather Vikash."

Kyle mulled that over as he turned down 34th, heading into university territory. Hard to get a good vibe from someone so reserved, but he finally decided that Soren — Vikash — was trying his best to be friendly. Maybe he was shy, or maybe he was seriously weird. Whatever. Kyle had been partnered with some real bastards over the years. Weird, he could deal with.

By the time Kyle had parked the white squad car, Vikash had finished his coffee, and like a good Mr. Perfect, took the empty cup and napkin with him and threw them away in the proper receptacles.

"Have you ever even had a parking ticket?"

Vikash gave him an odd look. "No. Why?"

"Never mind." Kyle led the way inside to where Detective Hardin was waiting for them. He nodded to the detective, who he'd worked with on the previous murder. "This look like the same?"

"'Fraid so. Wanted you to take a look, though, since you were on scene with the other one."

"Where was this one?"

"Just past the Waterworks. Some of the kids out at rowing practice found her."

There was always that moment of *oh, shit, I can't do this* for Kyle when he walked into a morgue with a body on the table. He'd seen a number of corpses as a cop, but he could never quite disassociate as some officers did. That was a person on the slab, someone's mom or sister, someone with dreams, who might have hated pistachio ice cream and might have stood near him at a fireworks display—and he had to stomp all those thoughts down hard.

Professional mask carefully in place, Kyle struggled not to flinch when the med tech pulled back the sheet. This young woman, like the previous victim, had deep, V-shaped gashes on her body, the one on her throat most likely the one that killed her.

"Doc's placing the time of death at between midnight and two." Hardin's raspy, smoke-ruined voice raked through the terrible stillness. "Blood loss from the neck wound listed as cause of death, though there's blunt force trauma to the head, too."

"Do we have an ID yet?"

"Nothing. Killer may have taken the purse if there was one."

"Any speculation on the weapon?" Kyle asked as he bent to examine the strangely shaped gashes.

"Almost looks like the shape of a bulb-planting trowel," Vikash murmured. He had produced a neat little notebook and pen, and was taking notes in quick, precise strokes.

Kyle stared at him. "Why is that a thing you know?"

Vikash muttered something about his grandmother before he added, "Those shouldn't be sharp enough for this, though."

"ME doesn't have any thoughts on the weapon." Hardin regarded Kyle's new partner with a sideways glance. "Gardening tools or otherwise. You have any doubts about this being related to the other one, Monroe?"

Kyle shook his head. "No. Same injuries. Time of death. Not the same area but still along the river. All right if we go take a look at the scene?"

"Joint investigation on this one, so go on down there. And don't hold out on me if you find something. I don't care if it's some weird, psychic thing you people don't think normal folks would understand."

That *you people* dig. Kyle's jaw tightened as his stomach did a slow roll. Four months ago, he hadn't been anything special. Just another cop doing his job. Now, he was one of *them*, one of the freaks the department employed to handle the bizarre, unexplainable crimes, a necessary, distasteful evil to many normal cops.

Vikash glanced up from his notebook, pen still poised over the page. "Was that a racist comment, Detective?"

Hardin sputtered. "What? Fuck, no. But your precinct's full of weirdos. You do know that, right?"

"I've no idea what you mean." Vikash's blank expression gave Hardin nothing to work with and Kyle wrestled down a laugh, nearly asphyxiating himself.

"All right, I think that's all we need here. I'll email updates," Kyle managed when he rediscovered breathing.

They left Hardin sputtering and Vikash remained nearly stoic when they got back in the car. The only change? That damn smile was back.

"You just like messing with people, don't you?"

"Yes." Vikash tucked his notebook away. Not even a chuckle. "To the crime scene?"

"Well, we're sure as hell not going to the Bat Cave." That got Kyle a strangled sound. Maybe *that* was a laugh, or Vikash was stifling a cough. "I'm calling in to see if Loveless and Zacchini can meet us there."

"Useful talents?"

"Sometimes."

Back across the river, back to the strange silence Kyle was still trying to break. He wished Vikash would make a little effort. Silence was fine, but not this weird, prickly silence.

"So was one of your parents from India?"

"No. Why?"

Kyle actually had to tighten his grip on the wheel to keep from smacking his partner. "Um...your first name?" *Your gorgeous, thick black hair. Your ridiculously beautiful skin. Your long, royal nose for looking down at people.*

"Mom thought it was a cool name."

"Uh-huh." Kyle wasn't buying it, but Vikash went back into statue mode and Kyle needed to recharge his social energies before trying to draw him out again.

There were forensics techs on the scene still, but Kyle got permission from them to nose around the edges. The body had been found at the river's edge, still half in the water. Photos at the time of recovery showed that the young woman had died in a moment of abject terror, her expression frozen with her dying scream.

They made their careful, sometimes sliding, way down the bank, eyes to the ground as they scanned for anything unusual and in deference to the treacherous footing.

Kyle slithered in the mud, flinging his arms out though there were no branches to catch here. A strong hand seized his elbow, steadying him. For a single heartbeat, Vikash's face showed anxious concern before his smug serenity returned.

"Maybe you and your stumpy legs should stay up top."

"Shut up." *Good one, Kyle. Really biting and witty.*

Any further witticisms were scuttled by Loveless' and Zacchini's arrival. In a broad-brimmed hat and gloves despite the mild weather, Loveless stood at the top of the embankment, mouth set in an unhappy line.

"Amanda, dear, you're going to have to help me if you expect to me to make it down there to Kyle."

Officer Zacchini rolled her eyes but took her partner around the waist, one hand clamped under his elbow to support his shaky steps down the bank. Vikash did the one eyebrow thing at Kyle.

"Vampire," Kyle whispered. "Daylight is really bad for him. But I think he likes the attention."

"You know I can hear you," Loveless said peevishly. "Want to tell me what I'm looking for?"

"Not sure. Any impressions of things that don't belong? Something that doesn't smell human?"

"On a riverbank. You are joking."

"Wish I could be specific. Don't have a lot yet."

Carrington Loveless III, silver spoon only child of a wealthy Main Line family, sighed as he gazed at his erstwhile clean shoes squishing on the marshy ground.

He closed his eyes and drew a deep breath in through his nose, crouched down, head turning, and breathed in again.

"There is…something." Loveless held his hand out and waited until Zacchini had a good grip on him before he stood. Sniffing like a narcotics dog, he walked several yards downriver and stopped. "Something odd."

"Kyle." Vikash pointed and took Loveless' other arm to prevent him taking another step. "There in the mud. Think we can get one of the crime scene guys to get some photos?"

With a hand clutching the back of Vikash's uniform jacket so he didn't tumble into the water, Kyle leaned over to see what had his colleagues in a frozen tableau. Right where water met land, with the river's wavelets working on washing it away, was a print from…something. Maybe. Four long gashes closer to the water with an oval impression behind them. If it was a footprint, the foot was larger than a kitchen sink.

"Carrington? Is it a print?" Kyle asked softly, as if a loud voice might wash it away.

"Yes. Oh, very much yes." Loveless shivered.

Kyle called over to the crime scene unit and soon had someone snapping photos. Not that it would help much if they couldn't figure out what the thing was, much less find it.

"Any thoughts on what?" Kyle asked their vampire. "What's it smell like?"

"Cold. Slimy. Hard."

"How can something smell hard?"

"I don't know," Loveless muttered irritably. "Amanda, I can't do this. Please."

Kyle glanced up at Zacchini, realizing with some irritation that everyone present was taller than he was.

"You picking up anything, Amanda? And is he drama queening?"

Zacchini shrugged. "I got nothin'. Water flowing. Things living in the mud. And no. He can't fake that gray color. I'd better get him in the car before he faceplants in the mud. You need piggyback, Carr?"

"No, no." Loveless tucked his hand into the crook of her offered arm. "I'll make it, thank you."

A quick survey of the ground nearby didn't turn up any more of the strange prints and when Kyle turned to suggest they go back up, he found Vikash staring after Loveless and Zacchini.

"What?"

Vikash hesitated before asking, "Are they a…thing?"

Christ on a cracker, is Mr. Perfect embarrassed? "Why, 'cause she's so careful with him?"

"Does she need to be careful?"

Kyle shrugged. "He's a little delicate, our vamp. Wasn't always, I hear. Decorated officer, amateur boxing titles before he was turned. But no, they're not a thing. He's more into Neanderthal jocks and she's into artistic, brooding women. They both get their hearts stomped on."

"Ah." Vikash started up the slope and Kyle thought that was the end of a long conversation for them until his partner spoke again, still in that puzzled tone, "I asked because I thought maybe she feeds him. If he does so badly in daylight."

"Ha. No. Remember, we're all kinda broken. Loveless can only drink skim blood. That's what he calls it. The packets he gets from the blood bank are labeled *washed RBC's*. No platelets, no plasma, low on the white blood count. He gets really sick on whole blood."

"I think I need a program. With footnotes."

"Nah. Small squad room. You'll know too much about everybody inside a week."

Chapter Two

"All the other Philly stations are districts. Why is this one a precinct?"

Back at the 77th, a shabbily converted brick manufacturing building from the neighborhood's better days, Kyle thought he was beginning to understand the long silences. Vikash seemed to process that way, turning things over and over before he asked questions.

"We're special. Don't really have one part of the city we're assigned to." Kyle eyed the building with renewed dismay as they walked up the partially crumbling steps. *Yeah, we're special all right.* "So they can't call us a district."

Too small to have a police captain in charge, with no motorcycle units, no dispatch, no real holding cells, they were on the bottom rung of any funding. He'd heard rumors that Loveless had donated the funds for extra squad cars and computers when there weren't enough to go around.

A whoosh of air ruffled Kyle's hair as he opened the door, Edgar's claws barely missing his scalp as he zipped by to perch on the old iron grillwork over the door.

"Ass dandruff!" Edgar croaked, fluffing his feathers to make himself twice as large and presumably menacing, though the effect was sadly more like a ratty piñata.

"He seems upset," Vikash said with a frown, somehow managing to twist his head to look back and still walk forward without stumbling.

Disgustingly graceful. Really, who does that? "Thank you, Captain Obvious," Kyle grumbled.

Krisk snorted and thumped his tail on the wall as they passed him on the way in, Wolf hurrying after.

"Hey, careful in the squad room," Wolf growled, half turning as he rushed past. "Virago's brought in some trouble."

The door slammed shut behind them and Kyle hesitated, listening. "Thanks for the specifics," he muttered.

"I think it's probably safe to go in." Vikash slid past him to continue down the grimy hallway. "No sounds of chaos."

While calm, the scene in the squad room was one of the more bizarre things Kyle had witnessed over the past few months. Virago sat in his chair, a vivid bruise starting on his cheek, typing up what could only be an arrest report, with Gatling perched on the edge of their shared desk. Between them, in the chair a suspect would take while he was being booked, was a leather jacket. Not odd if the jacket had behaved normally and stayed draped over a chair arm like a good, proper jacket, but this one was sitting up with the buckled strap on one sleeve cuffed to the chair arm. Virago asked the jacket something and Kyle could have sworn it made a gesture that was an approximation of flipping someone off.

"Um, what's this about?" Kyle called over from a safe distance.

"This jerk walked into one of the jewelers on Sansom." Virago pointed to the jacket. "Er, floated in. And starts stuffing shit in his pockets. He's on camera. We have tons of eyewitnesses, but he won't admit to a thing."

The jacket crossed its arms over its body, or got as close as it could with one sleeve cuffed to the chair, and gave Virago major attitude.

"You still had the gold chains in your pockets when we picked you up," Gatling pointed out.

With a shrug, the jacket subsided, somehow managing to look sullen.

"I'm gonna ask you one more time." Virago stabbed his finger at the jacket, getting in its face, so to speak. "Are you signing the statement or not, you stupid pile of leather scrap?"

The jacket quivered and sat up straighter. Kyle had the bad feeling it wasn't intimidated in the least. "This could get ugly," he whispered to Vikash.

His partner gripped his shoulder. "Stay put. We don't want the place burning down."

Everyone but Virago seemed to know what was coming. When the jacket lunged at him, toppling both chairs and taking him down to the floor, Vikash and Gatling both dove for the suspect. Virago cursed nonstop, his arms covering his head to protect it from the flailing sleeves. The smoke curling from his fingers signaled his attempt at a flame, but nothing materialized. Vikash got the jacket by the collar and heaved it off, turning and dodging gracefully as the jacket tried to twist and attack him.

"Settle down," he told the jacket calmly. "Officer Virago didn't mean that. You're excellent quality. I can tell. Completely badass leather jacket. But attacking people in the squad room doesn't help your case, now, does it?"

Kyle's mouth dropped open as the jacket stopped struggling, shoulders slumping. It remained calm as Vikash righted the chair and placed the jacket back on the seat. True to form, Virago didn't manage a thank you, glaring at Vikash as he picked himself off the floor.

"You and your new boyfriend find that killer yet, Kirby? Or were you spending the morning on bj's in the car?"

The hardening of Vikash's gaze happened so briefly Kyle thought he might have imagined the change along with the strange static hum he suddenly felt along his spine. But when Virago righted his chair and sat with a huff, the chair collapsed beneath him, shattering into its component pieces, nuts and washers rolling across the floor. The right legs of the desk cracked and broke while he was still gaping, its contents crashing to the cheap linoleum in sickening cracks of plastic and electronics.

Gatling sighed, offering a hand to help his partner up. "Maybe let me finish this up, Vance. Your nose is bleeding again."

"Well, fuck me." Virago stormed off to the bathrooms, leaving the now cooperative jacket to his partner.

"Not even with someone else's dick," Kyle muttered under his breath as he wandered back to his own desk to start writing that morning's report. He waited until Vikash had settled and removed his notebook from his pocket before he asked, "So was that you being angry?"

"That was me being mildly annoyed," Vikash answered, though he wouldn't look up. "I shouldn't have been. His pride was hurt and he was lashing out. And I never know what's going to happen."

Kyle opened his mouth, then stopped his first instinctive response to speak in his partner's defense. That was Vikash slightly miffed. He didn't want to think about what would happen in a moment of full-out rage. The calm Vikash wrapped around himself suddenly made a hell of a lot more sense. "Vance is a jerk. He needs to be medicated or something. But, yeah, he's not worth it."

About twenty minutes passed before Vikash looked up from his typing. *What now?*

"Was it just baiting, Kyle?" Blue eyes regarded him steadily, maybe even with some sympathy.

"You mean am I a fag?" *Honest question. Don't get pissy.* Kyle pulled in a slow breath. "I don't wave a Pride flag around, but I don't make a big secret of it. Virago's seen me out with other guys. It's not that big a city."

"It's still tough for a cop to be gay. I just don't want to see you bullied."

Kyle managed a crooked grin. "It's not grade school. And you know, somehow I've managed all this time without help."

"Of course."

"You have a problem with my fabulous gayness?"

"No." Vikash graced him with the statue smile. "I appreciate that you're honest with me." A full five minutes passed before Vikash raised his head again. "You think you're fabulous?"

"Of course I am," Kyle said, still typing. "I shit glitter and everything."

There was that strange, strangled sound again. If Vikash was laughing, Kyle was afraid that too much of it might kill him.

* * * *

Neither murder had any known witnesses, but Vikash agreed with Kyle that interviewing the people who had discovered the bodies was only being thorough. The last of the lingering clouds had cleared, and the autumn air was now suddenly warm enough to shed jackets.

"Mind if we grab something on the way?" Vikash asked as he slid back into the car.

Grab? Oh, damn. Lunch. Way to look out for your new partner, numb nuts. "Sure. There's stuff along the way."

"Burger King or something's fine. I'm not picky."

Great, the lieutenant had saddled him with a carnivore. Not that he often ate lunch, anyway. Too much of a hassle and he got too busy and forgot. Vikash sauntered inside when Kyle pulled up to the curb. When he returned with a bag, he offered Kyle one of the sandwiches of dubious meat.

"Um, thanks, no. I can't eat meat." Kyle reached into the glove compartment and fished out a Snickers bar.

"You want me to get you something else? Fish sandwich? Veggie burger? Salad?" Actual worry seemed to have crept into Vikash's expression. "You can't just have a candy bar."

"I sure as hell can. I'm a grown-up. I get to eat what I want." Kyle tried to amend his belligerent tone. "Nah, it's okay. I can't eat from somewhere like that. Who knows what they've grilled with what and what's in half the shit?"

"Strictly vegan?"

"No. I can't eat meat."

The little smile was back. "You're allergic or something?" Then Vikash's eyes widened. "Oh, crud. You are, aren't you?"

"Yeah. So?"

"So is it a runny nose, tearing-up, rash kind of allergic or *get me to the hospital before I die* kind? The *I have epi pens on hand* kind?"

"Geez. Settle down, Mom." Kyle couldn't help a chuckle, glad to see that Vikash could become more animated. "It's the rash kind if I touch it. The *you might have to call for an ambulance* kind if I eat it. Which is why I have to be careful."

"Just red meat? Was it a tick bite? I read about that happening."

Kyle shrugged. "Just started happening. It's any meat."

As they pulled back out into traffic, Vikash lapsed into silence, eating his lunch in small, overly civilized bites. *Wait for it…wait for it…*

"So how do you get your protein? Besides peanuts in candy bars?"

This was too bizarre. Kyle wasn't certain whether it was simply ravenous curiosity or whether Vikash really was worried for him. Stupid, of course. No one worried about someone he just met. "Cheese, milk, eggs—I can have all that stuff."

Vikash was shaking his head. "But instead of planning ahead, you scarf down a candy bar."

Kyle shrugged. "I get good takeout sometimes. Make peanut butter sandwiches. Don't cook much for myself, though. You know, you get home and you're beat. Who wants to make food?"

"You could come over some night. I'm happy to cook for company. Lots of good family recipes. Aloo gobi, some great curries, korma—"

Kyle gave him a sideways glance as he pulled through an intersection. "Wait. You said… You lied to me?"

Ice coated Vikash's voice as he said, "I don't lie."

Uh-oh. Kyle just had time to recall that pissing his partner off was a bad idea when that weird charged feeling raced up his spine again. A pop sounded. The car lurched and Kyle had to fight the wheel to keep from careening into oncoming traffic. "Damn it, Vikash."

His partner actually sank down in his seat while Kyle found a spot to pull over. "I'm sorry. I hope it was just one tire."

"Well, since you made it blow, you can get out and change it."

Vikash didn't utter a word in his defense as he got out of the car, walked around to check the tires and held up a single finger. All right. One tire was fixable. Kyle was ticked off enough that he wanted to sit in the damn car while Vikash struggled through changing the flat. But he watched his partner roll up his sleeves neatly and retrieve the jack and tire iron with the same serene grace that he did most things and damn it if he didn't feel like an asshole. With a sigh, he got out and lent his hand to getting the lug nuts loosened.

Even his biceps are perfect. Christ, those arms. Kyle did his best not to stare at the flex of long, lean muscle. There was even the hint of a tattoo peeking out under his left sleeve. "So what was that all about? Telling me your family's not from India?"

"You asked if one of my parents was." Vikash grunted as he pulled the tire off, the sound doing bad things for Kyle's concentration. "They're not. My dad's from Minneapolis. Born in Norway. My mom's from London. *Her* parents are from Bangalore."

"So you were just kinda messing with me."

"Yes."

"Could have just said so. Didn't have to break the car."

Vikash didn't respond to that and though his expression hadn't changed, something in the set of his shoulders broadcasted unhappiness. He was quiet until they were putting the jack into the trunk and wiping the grease off. "It shouldn't have been so strong. The...reaction. I wasn't even that annoyed. Maybe the glove compartment should have popped open, but a tire shouldn't have exploded."

"You do feel it. You just can't control it."

Vikash nodded. "It felt strange today. Almost a buzz, like feedback on an amplifier."

"Maybe it's me." Kyle leaped to the obvious conclusion.

"Then you'd be making bad things happen, right? If you absorbed my...the thing I do."

"Could be that it's different with you." Kyle cleared his throat and his face heated as soon as he realized how that sounded.

The statue smile returned and Kyle felt absurdly glad to see it. "Guess I just can't get angry around you," Vikash said as he closed up the trunk. "Could be dangerous."

"Yeah. Dangerous." Those intense blue eyes snagged Kyle for a breathless moment and he hoped he wasn't as red as he felt. *No. Just no. You're not that desperate and you're not that lonely. Not with your partner. He's got to be straight. Probably married. You'll meet the wife someday. We'll all be good friends.* "I'm sorry I called you a liar."

"Well, I'm sorry my brain blew up a tire, so we're even."

* * * *

By the time they had talked to both of the people who had found the bodies, Kyle was feeling the frustration he often did at the beginning of a case. Neither one could tell them anything they didn't already know. Every piece of the puzzle so far was a dead end. He gripped the steering wheel tightly enough to make it creak, the scars on the backs of his hands pulling as he tried to get his brain to cough up some brilliant stratagem.

"What happened to your hands?"

"Huh? Oh." Kyle startled and stared at the burn scars even though every ridge and shiny pucker was far too familiar by now. Lots of physical therapy, getting those hands working again. "I guess you wouldn't know the story since you weren't in the city when it happened. Lime Gelatin monster?"

Vikash's forehead actually crinkled in the most expressive response Kyle had yet to see. "Can't say it's familiar."

"They tried to keep it quiet, but you know department gossip." Kyle gave himself time for a deep breath, determined to keep the story short. "We got a call about some kind of ooze that was eating people's pets. Okay, I thought. Chemical spill. Until Mike and I actually got to the alley—"

"Your partner?" Those bright blue eyes were fixed on him intently and Kyle found it unnerving to have all of Vikash's attention.

"Um, yeah. Mike Powell. One of the better partners I had. Anyway, we got there and it wasn't a spill, it was this amoeba-like thing moving around back there, changing shape, and crawling over shit. It was…big. Maybe the size of a cow or thereabouts. And it'd just sucked in a cat. Poor kitty. We could see it, 'cause the thing was this clear green, like lime Jell-O. And the cat was stuck in there and, ah, disintegrating. Slowly."

"That's horrible."

"Yeah, really was. Something out of a bad horror movie. I don't know what Mike thought he was gonna do, but he rushed in there, maybe thinking he could contain it or maybe he wanted to save the cat. But the lime Jell-O reaches out this…arm—"

"Pseudopod?"

"*Thing* and gets hold of his foot." Kyle had to stop for another breath and to slam on the brakes to avoid running into the asshole in front of him who had spotted an empty parking space. "Turn signal, jackass! Anyway, Mike starts screaming, just unholy, bloodcurdling screams. He's on the ground. I'm seeing my partner getting sucked into this monster, and I guess my brain turned off, too."

"You tried to get his foot out."

Kyle swallowed hard, flexing his fingers at the phantom pain the memory induced. "Like the shit for brains that I am, I tried to get his foot out. The slime had already eaten through Mike's boot. I grabbed his ankle, thinking I could just yank him free. The pseudo thingy just reached around and swallowed my hands, too. And holy fuck, it hurt. Spilled acid on your skin in chemistry class hurt, except, like super acid."

Vikash spoke into the fraught silence, softly encouraging. "But it didn't eat you."

"No. This weird thing happened. It still burned, but the monster started to get smaller. And I started to feel nauseous. I got really hot. It felt like my insides were burning. Then it hit me. I was absorbing the Jell-O monster, not the other way around. Now I was screaming, too, completely freaked, right? And Mike's screaming. And the people gawking from the end of the alley are screaming."

"Understandable."

"Ha. Thanks." Kyle shook his head, trying for some distance from the memory. "It couldn't have taken more than a couple of minutes. My body absorbed the damn thing. Like Kirby. My hands were burned all to hell. Mike had lost part of his foot. And I was sick for days. Puking up this acidy gunk."

"Thank you for the visual."

"No problem. That's how I got transferred. Internal Affairs sent these special 'doctors' to talk to me, run some tests, and when they discharged me from the hospital, the captain tells me I'm going to the 77th."

Kyle let his partner have his silence then, though his curiosity itched to know what part of the story Vikash had fastened on for extra processing. Vikash finally stirred out of his reverie when they pulled up to the station.

"Do they still hurt?"

That's your takeaway? Really? Though Kyle found the question oddly touching. "They ache sometimes. It's hard to maintain a grip after a while, like if I'm using a hammer or a pen for too long. But it's not bad. My mom still says she can't decide whether I was brave or a dumbass."

Vikash gave him a little shoulder bump as he came around the car. "Most brave things are stupid. If you were being smart, thinking about self-preservation, you wouldn't have saved your partner."

Maybe it was a snowball effect, all the observations over the course of a long, strange day, but Kyle abandoned trying to hate his partner after that statement. Maybe he was perfect and standoffish, but how could you hate someone who was so damn nice?

Chapter Three

The final coroner's report arrived the next morning in Kyle's email and added nothing helpful to what they already knew. He was reading it for the twentieth time when he was startled out of his morose reverie by Vikash pulling open his sticky desk drawer that only cooperated with a hard yank and a shriek of metal on metal.

"Sorry," Vikash murmured as he began to pull out plastic containers and set them up on the desk, one after another until there were seven containers, two rectangular, sandwiched-sized, and the rounds ones about the size of the smallest cream cheese tubs.

Kyle peered around his computer screen at the plastic parade. "Um...what're all those?"

"Did you pack lunch?"

"Well...yeah." After the mini-lecture the day before, Kyle had figured it was less painful to bring a damn sandwich than to deal with Vikash's disapproval again.

"Good." Vikash replaced one of the large containers and started handing the smaller ones around to Kyle.

"Still not an answer," Kyle muttered as he accepted the fifth container and lined them up in front of his keyboard. He eased off the first lid and took a cautious sniff. *Mint? Maybe?*

"Chutneys."

It was an answer, finally, but not an explanation. Kyle closed his eyes and took three deep breaths to let his irritation sink into the floor. This was Kash communication. He needed make some mental adjustments and learn how to work with it.

His curiosity overrode irritation anyway as he removed the rest of the lids to reveal white, orange, bright red and a sort of butter-colored mystery substance. "So, chutneys. Different kinds. Why do I have all these? Should I close my eyes and shuffle them around? Is it a test or something?"

Vikash graced him with a little smile, and sure, he still looked like a smug, perfect statue, but his eyes were lit with warm amusement.

God, he's gorgeous. If we'd met in a bar or a coffee shop, I'd probably ask him personal stuff right off. Even ask him out. Not fair he's my partner and probably not gay anyway.

To be honest, while he hadn't pinged on Kyle's gaydar even a smidge, he hadn't set off the straight radar either. Vikash didn't ogle anyone, ever. No drooling over celebrities of any gender. No comments about hotness walking down the sidewalk. Kyle was starting to suspect that it was more than oversocialized politeness, and if the guy was Ace, he wasn't likely to come out and say so to his new partner.

"You can close your eyes if you want to. Just try them."

"Okay?" Kyle accepted the plastic spoon Vikash handed him and tried the green one first. Mint and basil goodness caressed his tongue. "Damn, that's…yum.

Am I being a guinea pig? Not that I mind. You can bring me stuff to try anytime if it's all this wonderful."

"Focus, Monroe. If you come for dinner, I have to know what you like."

That almost sounded suggestive. Kyle shook his head to clear out all the stray, inappropriate thoughts. "Hey, I'm a flavor whore. Not much I don't like. So long as it isn't trying to kill me, I'm good."

Instead of answering, Vikash waved a hand at the open containers, the simple gesture regal and amused.

"You know this is weird, right?" Kyle asked after a second spoonful of green.

One perfect black eyebrow arched as the statue smile slipped a hair. "Too weird?"

"Nah. Just enough. You'd have to try a lot harder for too weird in here." Kyle gave him what he hoped was a charming grin before he dove into the remaining chutneys, from sweet to savory to spicy, all delicious. "I sure as hell hope you're not asking me to pick a favorite. 'Cause I can't. Normally, I'd say I'm not big on the raw onions in the red one, but it's addictive."

Vikash's smile regained a couple of watts and he opened his larger container, releasing the heavenly scent of cheesesteak. Of all the meat things Kyle couldn't have any longer, only that one still made him drool. He found he'd leaned forward unconsciously to get closer to the stomach-rumbling smell when a flurry of nightmare-bright feathers bumped into his face on landing.

"Gimme!" Edgar croaked.

"Oh." Vikash paused in the act of unwrapping his sandwich, glancing between Kyle and the raven. "Should I?"

"Don't encourage him. He'll start in with everyone else if you do." Kyle waved a hand. "Go on, Edgar. Get!"

Edgar spread his wings and snapped at Kyle's hand. "Your dick fits in a toothpaste tube!"

"Well—" Kyle sputtered on a mouthful of wing as Edgar took off for his perch. "Yours is smaller!"

"Good one," Vikash murmured around an overly civilized bite.

"Oh, shut up. Do birds even have dicks?"

"Not like yours...um, ours."

Kyle jerked his head to the side to see around the screens to find Vikash frowning at his sandwich, carefully rearranging bits of onion. No way he was blushing. That had to be a trick of the light. He was so intent on Vikash, Kyle missed the presence behind his partner until a soft whine came from that side of the desk.

One hand loosening his uniform tie, Wolf stood just behind Vikash. At noon, his five o'clock shadow was already coming in, a bit of drool hanging from a too-sharp canine, and combined with the intense voracity in his eyes, he might have appeared threatening if he hadn't been so single-mindedly focused on Vikash's cheesesteak.

"Wolf?" Vikash's expression had gone entirely blank.

"That smells...so good," Wolf rasped, his voice halfway between a snarl and a whine.

Slowly, without taking his eyes off Wolf, Vikash broke off a quarter of his sandwich and handed it to Wolf with exaggerated care, along with a napkin from a ridiculously neat stack of them in his top desk drawer. For his part, Wolf accepted the offering with an almost spiritual reverence, then devoured it with unholy glee.

Kyle had concerns over the napkin's chances, but it survived the assault.

He was just about to tell Vikash what a bad idea feeding fellow officers was and to tell Wolf off for begging when Krisk stomped by on his way in from the break room. He seized the back of Wolf's collar in one scaled fist and yanked him along as Wolf yelped and scrabbled backward. When they reached their own pair of desks, Krisk slammed his tail on the floor and pointed to Wolf's side of the desk. Chastised, Wolf hung his head and slumped in his chair with a whimper.

Kyle waited to see if Krisk would produce a rolled-up newspaper to smack Wolf on the nose. He realized he was staring when Vikash's next muttered words startled him.

"Peanut butter."

"What?" Kyle wrenched his attention back to his own corner of the squad room.

"I should stick to peanut butter if we eat at our desks."

"Hmm, nope." Kyle reached for his ringing phone. "Wolf loves peanut butter, too... Seventy-seventh. Officer Monroe."

"Get yourself out to the Waterworks, Monroe," Lieutenant Dunfee growled in his ear. "Just got a report of a suspicious person from one of the staff."

"Any connection to the Schuykill murderer, ma'am?"

"That's the kind of thing I pay you to find out. Get your freckled white butt moving."

Telling the lieutenant that the city paid them, or asking how she knew his ass had freckles, both seemed like suicidally bad ideas. "Yes, ma'am."

"Lead?" Vikash asked, his lunch remnants already stowed and his various containers neatly stashed away.

"Possibly. We have to see someone about a suspicious person."

The silence on the drive over to the Waterworks was definitely a processing one, so Kyle waited. Vikash didn't disappoint.

"So Wolf and Krisk?"

Kyle let out a sharp laugh. "*There's* an image I didn't need. I don't think so? But hell, who knows. I've never seen Wolf out with anyone. And I've never seen Krisk outside of work, now that I think about it."

"Interesting," Vikash murmured, though his expression was back to inscrutable.

The old Waterworks gleamed in white neoclassical splendor as they pulled into the closest parking spot. When the sun hit the buildings just right, they were near blinding. Not always the case. Kyle remembered when the buildings were sad, crumbling piles, but the partial restoration had been miraculous, and while the old pumps no longer provided the city's water, they were pretty damn cool as a historic site.

Their contact was one of the security guards for the facility, an older woman whose duties were probably more along the lines of opening doors and directing school groups, but her sharp eyes snapped volumes at them before she said a word.

"All the experienced officers busy or something?"

"Ma'am?" Kyle's rhythm was shot all to hell by that question.

"You two look like you're barely out of school."

Not at all flustered, Vikash gave her a hint of a smile. "Which one is older, ma'am?"

She snorted. "You are, obviously."

"No, ma'am." Vikash pointed with this pen, already out with this notebook at the ready. "Officer Monroe is. It's hard to judge sometimes."

"Huh. Well, I guess you'll have to do."

"We appreciate the vote of confidence," Kyle said, hoping the sarcasm hadn't leaked out through his ears. "You told dispatch you saw some suspicious activity?"

She nodded, lips pursed as she waved around the building to the far side, away from the sun-drenched gazebo. "It was this morning. Fog was still sitting on the banks like it does sometimes. But down there—" She pointed to a spot on the bank. "That's where he was, digging in the mud."

"Did you recognize him?"

"Hell no." Her short-cropped silver hair glinted in the sun as she tilted her head at Kyle. "Do I look like I know people who go digging around in river muck?"

"Um, no, ma'am." Kyle cleared his throat, trying desperately to get his interviewing feet back under him. "Can you describe him, please?"

"Couldn't see much. Couldn't really say how tall he was since he was down there. Had a black knit hat on. Looked like a white boy to me."

"What else did you notice, ma'am?" Vikash asked while he scribbled in his notepad.

For Vikash, she pursed her lips, thinking. "He was wearing one of those Eagles jackets."

"The green nylon kind?" Kyle asked and snapped his mouth shut when she glared at him.

"No." The *you fool* was implied, she didn't even have to say it. "Don't interrupt. It was one of those, what do you call the damn things? Varsity jackets. The wool with the leather sleeves. Those things. It was black. The wool part. Had an eagle patch on the front."

Vikash stopped scribbling. "This was early in the morning. Why did you wait to report it?"

She shrugged. "Didn't think much of it. I yelled at him and he took off. Down the bank, then up by the museum. Didn't see anything down there, so I got on with my day until one of the girls said something about murders along the river here. And it got me thinking."

Kyle shut up since she had taken such an obvious dislike to him, but he gestured with his head toward the river. Vikash, bless him, caught on right away.

"Has anyone been down there to take a look, ma'am?"

"Not yet, no."

Vikash flipped his notebook shut and tucked it back into his shirt pocket as he leaned out over the railing. "Bit steep. We could go around."

"Should be a line in the trunk," Kyle said, his ego stinging a bit from being treated like a teenager in front of Vikash. If he was honest with himself, it was the in front of Vikash part that stung, and if it made him want to do something stupidly macho, that was understandable. Right?

After a long stare down his perfect, regal nose, Vikash let out a barely audible sigh and strode back to the squad car. He returned with the nylon line and a completely expressionless face. He wrapped one end behind his back, let the other drop over the railing and nodded to Kyle.

"Just warn me when you're coming back up."

Kyle hesitated. The drop-off looked suddenly steeper and higher up. Not that he was going to kill himself falling into river mud. Probably. "You sure?"

"I can hold you."

Was that...? No. Vikash meant exactly what he said. Kyle clambered over the railing and used the rope to steady himself on the way down. It still wasn't a pleasant descent through the weeds and muck, but he managed not to face-plant. With Mrs. Kerns shouting directions, he squelched farther down the bank until he found a spot where the weeds had been disturbed. A quick glance around didn't provide a rock or piece of broken plastic to dig with, but a good-sized stick was poking up out of the mud just at the waterline.

"Longer arms…would be good…about now…" Kyle snagged the end and yanked at it, clutching at the rope when he overbalanced and flinging mud everywhere when the stick pulled free with an obscene *slorp*. Yes. Mrs. Kerns was laughing at him. He would just have to ignore that.

With the stick as an impromptu probe, he dug at the churned up spot in the weeds, trying not to think too hard about what he might find. A corner of plastic soon protruded from the muck and Kyle pulled a yellow marker from his pocket to indicate the spot. The river mud released his foot sullenly, hanging on for all it was worth as he reached forward, and Kyle gritted his teeth as his forward boot sank ankle-deep into the ooze.

What emerged was worth the struggle, though — a glimpse of a Ziploc bag containing several smaller bags of white powder. He marked the site and was about to call to Vikash to brace for his climb up when something caught his eye. A little farther up the bank where the ground was drier, he spotted an indentation in the mud, a V-shaped indentation.

"Vikash! We're gonna need forensics down here!"

"All right," Vikash called down. "But come up first."

Easier said than done. His damn boot was stuck tight. "You're gonna have to pull."

Kyle wrapped the rope around his wrist, expecting Vikash to start hauling away. Instead he poked his head over the side.

"Are you all right?"

"Fine. Just…the mud's trying to eat my foot."

"I…see."

Damn him and his understated amusement. Kyle tugged on the line impatiently and Vikash braced himself backward, hauling the rope up slowly, hand over hand. The riverbank finally gave up Kyle's foot with the boot still attached, though it was a close thing, and he started the climb back up the bank, mostly pulled by Vikash's ridiculously sexy arms.

"Our varsity jacket man was making a drop," Kyle said through gasps as he held the bag up for Vikash. "And there's an indentation in the mud down there. V shaped."

"Ah." Without another word, Vikash jogged off to the squad car to call it in.

"That's a lot of horse," Mrs. Kerns said dryly.

Kyle frowned at his mud-caked shoes. "Does anyone really still call it that? And how do you know what it is?"

"Call it a good guess." She pointed to the stone railing that ran along the edge of the Waterworks courtyard. "Go stand over there and drip. You're getting mud all over my nice clean flagstones."

Kyle could have argued that they weren't her flagstones, but he did as she asked since it got him out of the way of a departing school group. When Vikash returned, he brought an evidence bag that he held open so Kyle could drop in the muddy bag of drugs, and a garbage bag.

"What's that for?" Kyle pointed to the black plastic. "Is it to hide a body? Are we murdering Mrs. Kerns?"

"No. But you'd fit."

"Hilarious."

Vikash pointed to Kyle's boots. "For those."

"Oh, come on. Just get me a stick or something and I'll scrape the mud off."

"Your feet have to be soaked." Vikash pointed again. "And the mud stinks."

Kyle rolled his eyes. "I'll hose off when we get back."

While Vikash's expression hardly changed, his eyes narrowed. He draped the garbage bag over the railing then suddenly turned away from the rail and seized Kyle's leg around the knee, nearly knocking him off his perch on the rail.

"Hey! What the fuck, Soren!"

"Hold still," Vikash gritted out as he yanked open Kyle's laces and jerked the mud-caked boot off. The sock came halfway off with it and Vikash tugged that off as well before Kyle could do much more than cuss and flail. Vikash dropped the purloined boot and sock in the garbage bag and held it open for Kyle with a triumphant gleam in his eyes.

"Big huge fucking flag on the play, Soren," Kyle grumbled. "That was definitely nonconsensual shoe removal."

"I didn't hear *no* or *stop*." Vikash gave the bag a shake in Kyle's direction. "So removal with dubious consent at the very worst. Stop being such a baby."

"What am I supposed to do? Drive back to the precinct barefoot?"

"I'll drive, and I have extra socks in the car."

Kyle blinked. "You...what?"

"You never know what's going to happen on a call. I always have extra clothes." Vikash had the gall to look smug when Kyle dropped the second boot and sock into the bag. "But the socks are the only things of mine that would fit you."

"Not the time for short jokes, Soren. So not the time."

A tiny smile tugged at Vikash's lips as he gave Kyle's feet a once over. "They're pretty nice feet. Though I'm surprised they're not hairy."

It was a good thing for Vikash that the lab techs arrived then or Kyle was sure he would've had a scathing retort that would've shut him up for the rest of the afternoon. Maybe. Probably not. He was still stuck on Vikash saying he had nice feet.

Chapter Four

The lab boys and girls were still combing through the findings from the site two days later. There had been a second bag of heroin Kyle had missed, a partial boot print farther down the bank, and of course a few zillion photos to pore over. While the street value of the drugs was substantial and Kyle would be glad to get the douchewaffle off the streets, it was the photo of the V-shaped mark in the mud that had his attention.

"It's the same, isn't it?" He peered over Vikash's shoulder where his computer screen showed the photo of the mud V and the V-shaped wound on one of the murder victim's necks.

"Hard to say," Vikash said softly. "Roughly the same shape. The size doesn't quite match up, but the mud may have distorted it."

"It's not even a quarter inch difference. It's the same."

"Similar enough to be suspicious," Vikash finally conceded. He'd had to verify exact measurements from the coroner's report and the lab report first, of course.

Kyle leaned a hip against the desk, absolutely stymied over what to do next. "Too much to ask for prints, I guess."

"Sara says they're still working on the bag, but the mud probably erased them."

They both stared at the photos in silence. Kyle wished Vikash would stop chewing on his bottom lip. Damn distracting. The find had seemed so promising, but all they'd managed was to manufacture another dead end for themselves. Informants hadn't come up with anyone to match the bits of description they had and the APB hadn't turned up anything either. Not surprising, with so little information.

"Who are you?" Kyle murmured at the screen.

Vikash pulled out his notebook and flipped it open. "Probably male. High probability of someone young."

"How do you figure that?"

"The terrain. You had trouble with it."

Kyle snorted. "That better not be a crack about my age. But I get what you're saying. More likely somebody young and fit."

"Fairly distinctive varsity jacket."

"Yeah. Doesn't mean he wears it everywhere."

"Possibly." Vikash tipped his chair back to glance up at Kyle. "But he wore a six-hundred-dollar jacket down to the riverbank. Don't you think he would've worn something else if he could have?"

"Good point. Maybe. Could be his lucky jacket or something." Kyle couldn't help being surprised that Vikash was suddenly so talkative, but it *was* about the case and not personal stuff. Probably made a difference. "The stash was too big for personal use. But not big enough for one of the serious suppliers. Dealer?"

Vikash shook his head slowly. "Unlikely. If he was dealing, he'd want to be able to get to his product. He wouldn't set up shop in such an out of the way place. A mule?"

"That makes more sense. He was dropping off a shipment for a dealer to come collect later. So we probably have some small-time guy playing mule for extra cash. Why would he be killing people?"

"Wrong place, wrong time?" Vikash suggested, though he didn't sound convinced.

"Maybe. But he ran from Mrs. Kerns instead of confronting her. And those murders were vicious. If for some godforsaken reason he's using a gardening trowel to kill people, that's gotta take some effort."

"Small fish with big grudges."

"Could be. If we knew who he was, we could start connecting dots."

Vikash smacked Kyle's knee with his notepad. "Time for us to get out there."

"Yeah. All right. We're just spinning our wheels in the mud here."

"No. That's you."

Kyle glanced at him sideways while he grabbed his jacket. "What's that supposed to mean?"

"You're the mud expert."

"I think I liked you better when you didn't say anything," Kyle muttered. It was a huge lie, of course. Vikash's sense of humor was a little strange, sometimes, but he had one, more than Kyle could say of several previous partners. If Kyle were being honest, he'd have to admit that he liked the strange part, too.

While they did have an assigned patrol route, it was a tactical division of the city rather than a mandatory daily routine. Today, instead of taking their route closer to city hall, Kyle headed south. There were people in the old neighborhoods he could talk to, people who could keep an eye out.

He maneuvered them through the stop-and-go traffic on South Street and turned on Ninth to head down to the Italian Market. Another precinct cruiser sat in front of Giordano's. He didn't even need the number on the car to know whose it was.

"Damn. Virago's here," Kyle grumbled.

Vikash gave a hint of a shrug. "Maybe they've seen something."

"Just keep him away from me. I don't want the produce bins going up in flames."

Kyle found a mostly legal parking space a little too close to the corner and spotted Jeff Gatling talking to one of the flower sellers a few yards down the street. The market was in full Saturday afternoon swing, all the regular shops and outdoor vendors hustling to keep up with customers. Vikash scanned the crowd while Kyle leaned against a support post, waiting for Jeff to finish.

"Hey." Jeff raised a hand and ambled toward him. "You're out of your jurisdiction, Monroe."

"Hilarious. Just came over to ask a couple contacts about our suspicious person from this morning. Everything all right?"

Jeff lifted his hat to scratch his head. "Just checking on some complaints that were funneled down to us from the districts. Mrs. Morelli says she saw our jacket."

"You mean the kind with the leather sleeves? The guy we're looking for?"

"No, the floating leather jacket dude we have in lockup. Apparently, he's been quite the shoplifter."

"Huh." Not what Kyle had wanted to hear, but he had to wonder how long the animated jacket had been on his little crime spree.

A few feet away, Mrs. Morelli obviously overheard them, even though she claimed she was mostly deaf when it suited her. "That damn jacket stole good silver vases. Three of them! What a jacket wants with vases, I couldn't tell you. Does he want to give them to his peacoat girlfriend? You gonna do something about that menace, officer?"

"We're doing the best we can, ma'am," Jeff answered patiently. He looked like he had more to say but Mrs. Morelli cut him off.

"Is that Kyle? Little Kyle Monroe?"

Kyle glared at Vikash when he snickered. "It's me, Mrs. Morelli. I was wond —"

Mrs. Morelli put a hand on one bony hip. "So why don't you ever come by? You too good for us now?"

"No, ma'am. Just don't have a lot of time with the job and —"

"Job, he says. Ha! Danny McCord's a cop, too. He comes to see us."

"Yes, ma'am. I'll try to do better." Kyle realized he'd taken off his uniform hat and was twisting it in his hands. Old habits just refused to curl up and die sometimes. "I was wondering if you've seen a different jacket around. One actually being worn by someone. An Eagles jacket —"

"Sweetie, I see a hundred Eagles jackets any given weekend. What *kind* of Eagles jacket?"

I was getting to that. "A varsity jacket. Letterman. Whatever you want to call —"

"The green ones with the white sleeves? Those are ugly."

Kyle forced his smile to stay put. It was threatening to slide off into the carnations. *One sentence. Please. Just let me finish one.* "Not the green ones. This one's black with tan —"

"Like that one there." Mrs. Morelli pointed with her chin across League Street where a man wearing the type of jacket in question was just leaving Carl's Farm Eggs. His hands were tucked in his pockets, his head down.

Vikash had started in his direction when a woman in heels burst through the same door, yelling, "Hey! Asshole! Gimme back my phone! That dickwad took my phone!"

The man took off, and without hesitation, Vikash sprinted after him, weaving through the crowd with the grace of a dancer from the Bolshoi. Kyle would've followed, but Jeff's hand landed on his shoulder.

Handing Kyle three oranges from the produce stand next door, Jeff said, "Your partner works too hard. You've been standing next to me for a bit, right? Follow my lead, Officer Kirby."

Kyle took half a second to catch up, in which Jeff had begun to teleport the oranges he held and Vance had barreled out of the panaderia across the street in pursuit of the suspect. Gaze locked firmly on the suspect, Kyle concentrated on his oranges, hyperaware of their nubbly skin against his palms, and *thought* about sending them on ahead.

The oranges vanished from his hands only a breath later than the ones teleporting out of Jeff's hands. It should have been easy. Send the oranges under the suspect's feet, trip him up, and let Vikash catch up. In theory, that one thing and only that one thing should have happened. Instead, several ancillary things happened to accompany Jeff's oranges materializing under the suspect's feet to send him flailing and careening to his hands and knees.

Kyle's first orange smacked into a Mercedes with such force that it splattered all over the back window and set off the car alarm. The second clipped Vikash's ear, which caused Mr. Perfect to wince and duck but not to lose a single step. The third decided on the truly disastrous course of reappearing under Vance's left boot. The firestarter didn't have even a thimbleful of Vikash's grace and when the front of his boot met orange and the orange rolled, he went down hard.

"Fuck!" Vance bellowed. "What the hell, Jeff?"

Jeff called back, "Easy, Virago! Not my fault." He started to move through the crowd to where Vikash had the suspect on the ground while he muttered, "Not entirely."

Hesitating, Kyle waffled between going to assist his partner or to help Vance up, though approaching an enraged Vance was probably a bad idea. Probably because he was still focused on both oranges and Vance, a dozen more oranges suddenly materialized in the air above Vance's head and fell on him in a flood like Mr. Moose's ping-pong balls used to on Captain Kangaroo. Smoke began to rise from Vance's jacket as his face turned a shade of scarlet that definitely clashed with the oranges. In possibly his only wise decision of the day, Kyle hurried down the sidewalk to Vikash.

The suspect, sullen and glaring, stood against the wall of a shop, hands cuffed behind him, stolen cell phone beside him, while Jeff Mirandized and Vikash did a quick pat down.

"Looked like he was going for that car." Vikash nodded toward a dark green Mustang parked around the corner.

Kyle tipped his hat back, trying to match his partner for expressionlessness. "That your car, sir?"

"Fuck, no," Varsity Jacket, a pasty character with blotchy skin and dirty blond hair, spat out. "And I didn't take that chick's phone, neither. She's a psycho."

"He got keys on him, Soren?" Kyle asked casually.

"Does appear to have a set." Vikash drew them out of the man's left hand jacket pocket. Without moving his head, Vikash pointed the rectangular key fob at the car and hit 'unlock'. The Mustang obligingly blinked its lights and clicked its locks open.

"Hey! You can't do that!" Varsity protested.

"And this phone you were carrying, sir? You're saying it's yours?" Kyle picked up the smart phone. The screen had gone into lock mode.

"Yeah, it's mine. This is, like, unlawful detainment."

"What's your code to unlock it, and when I do, what's your background look like?"

"It's…" The suspect hesitated, his eyes shifting back and forth. "I forget. You guys make me nervous."

"Uh-huh." Kyle gestured down the street. "I'll just go ask the woman who says you stole her phone the same questions, all right?"

"No, wait! It was just a joke, all right? Just a gag. She's just got no sense of humor. Never did. You know how chicks are."

Vikash raised both eyebrows at the appeal to misogyny and strolled back down the sidewalk to where Vance had picked himself up and was controlling his matchbox temper enough to talk to the woman in question. Just to annoy their liar of a suspect, Kyle talked over his head to Jeff about inane things like the weather and whether dogs should wear coats while they waited patiently.

After a few moments and a short discussion during which the woman didn't show even the tiniest bit of amusement, Vikash strolled back. "The owner of the cell phone states she doesn't know this man and that, I quote, *even if it was a stupid joke, he still stole the freaking phone.*"

"Gentlemen, I believe we have probable cause." Kyle held out his hand for the key fob and clicked open the trunk. "Anything in there you'd like to tell me about, sir?"

Varsity had clamped his lips shut, a visible twitch in his jaw. The scattering of cell phones in an old red milk crate didn't shock Kyle. Their guy wasn't a terribly organized thief, but he apparently was a busy one. What caught his eye and made his pulse skip a beat was the implement peeking out from a canvas roll near the back of the trunk. Carefully, he took a pen from his pocket and lifted a corner of the canvas.

"Vikash, you see this?"

Looming over Kyle's shoulder, Vikash spoke nearly in his ear. "I see it. Red residue could be blood. Should I call it into Third District?"

"Yep." Kyle leaned farther into the trunk, both to move away from Vikash's voice that was sending shivers down his spine and to get a better look at the gardening trowel, an elongated one with deep sides and a sharp end. "Human perpetrator. No monsters. No paranormal weirdness. This is outside our mandate."

Vikash nodded and jogged back to their squad car to call it in.

Damn, he has a fine ass. And no way in hell do I have any business thinking that about my partner. My probably straight-as-a-Popsicle-stick partner.

While Jeff put Varsity in his squad car to await the transfer of suspect and possible evidence, Vance finally caught up with them, brushing bits of pulp off his sleeves. He pointed a shaking, smoldering finger at Kyle. "You. You did that on purpose, you smarmy little faggot."

"Hey! I resent being called smarmy. I'm quite disparaging, thanks."

Vance's eyes narrowed. "You…what?"

"Look, I'm sorry. Jeff handed me oranges and I thought I could help. Kinda dumb since I never have great control over the stuff I pick up from someone else. Speaking of which, you should probably back up a step or we're gonna end up calling the fire department, too."

"Damn it," Vance spat out, but he did back off. "Why do you have to be such a first-class *freak*, Monroe?"

"As opposed to the rest of you second-class freaks?" Kyle chuckled despite his irritation. "I'll pay for the cleaners, Virago. Chill."

Vance was still glaring and muttering when Jeff and Vikash rejoined them after dealing with the officers from the Third. Jeff clapped him on the shoulder and grimaced when he came away with pulp on his palm.

"Cheer up. It's just oranges. Which I paid for. You're welcome." Jeff grinned as he wiped his hand off on a napkin. "At least you won't stink up the squad car with skunk this time."

"Damn it, Gatling. Shut. Up."

The temptation almost killed Kyle, but he managed not to ask about the skunk incident. After giving Jeff ten bucks to cover the bulk of the orange loss, technically his fault, he and Vikash were back in the squad car headed to their assigned streets.

"No monster." Vikash finally spoke as they passed city hall.

Kyle risked a quick glance over as they rounded the corner by Wanamaker's. *Fine. Macy's.* It was always going to be the Wanamaker building to him. Vikash almost looked like he was slumping. "You sound disappointed."

"We had a footprint. It seemed so likely."

"Yeah, that print. I'm sure we have a river monster. But it looks like the murders were a human thing. I'm okay with not having a *murderous* river monster."

"Hmm."

Kyle waited, but there wasn't anything forthcoming to expand on that. "Hmm? What hmm? Hmm, you think humans are scarier than monsters? Hmm, you think I shouldn't be jumping to conclusions before the lab boys and girls have a look at that trowel? Hmm, you think that guy we just passed shouldn't be wearing yellow sneakers with brown pants?"

"Yes."

"Well, all right then. Glad we cleared that up." Kyle hung a right on Filbert and at the Thirteenth Street intersection, decided he wasn't getting anything more on the subject. "You were serious about having me over for dinner?"

Vikash arched an eyebrow, as close to surprise as he could manage, apparently. "I am."

"Okay. It's nice of you. I mean, you don't have to."

"Friday. Come around six. Ellie and I would love to have you."

Ellie… That cleared that up, too. Kyle kept the smile glued on so hard it hurt his face. "Cool. Thanks. I'll be there."

He drove on, for once grateful for the silence as he pummeled his disappointment back into the dark box where it belonged. He had no right and no reason to resent Ellie, the wife or girlfriend of this gorgeous, quirky man. None at all. There would be dinner, Kyle would be charming, and they would all be the best of friends.

Chapter Five

Friday evening, Kyle stood outside Vikash's apartment building, waffling. Nice place, one of those Southwest Philly apartment communities with gardens and a dog park—certainly was a step or five up from his shabby apartment on South Street. He could have a better place, too, since he lived alone and didn't have any need to live close to his work anymore. Just hadn't bothered to move yet.

It wasn't that he felt out of place, but he was nervous. He and his new partner had gotten along well so far, discovering that they liked the same movies and TV shows, that they were both indifferent sports fans and both actually read fiction. But Kyle still had no idea if Vikash was married or had kids or if he went to church on Sundays. When they communicated, Kyle still talked and Vikash still responded with a handful of words, or entire sentences if he was feeling generous.

Kyle mentally squared his shoulders, tugged at the sleeves of the green crewneck sweater he'd picked as non-date wear, walked up to the bright red door set in the cozy two-story brick and rang the buzzer. There wasn't an intercom, so he had to wait for Vikash's footsteps to lope down the stairs and presumably for him to check through the peephole before the door opened. Wonderful cooking smells wafted out around Vikash's serene smile.

"Hey. Hungry?"

"Starved. Thanks for having me over." Kyle kept quiet as they went upstairs, head cocked, listening for signs of any other occupant.

When Vikash closed the apartment door behind him, he had one eyebrow raised. "What?"

"Oh. Um." *Where's your girl? Crap. No. That sounds bad.* "Isn't Ellie home?"

"Yes."

Kyle was about to say something cranky when a white puffball dashed across the room to hide under a chair.

With a nod to the chair, Vikash said, "This is Ellie."

"Doesn't like strangers, huh?" Kyle chuckled, telling himself he had no reason to feel relieved. That nothing had changed. Vikash was still straight and he just didn't have anyone living with him right now. "Sorry, Ellie."

"She'll come out later." Vikash wandered through the front room, presumably to the kitchen where all the good scents were gathered. "Want a beer?"

"Hell, yeah. Just one, though. Have to drive back."

Vikash nodded and handed him a Dogfish Head from the fridge. "Small people do have to be more careful."

"Oh, fuck off." Kyle backhanded his partner's arm. They'd gotten that comfortable, at least. "Enough with the damn short jokes."

With a strangled snicker sound, Vikash meandered to the stove where he adjusted temps, stirred and added ingredients in far too professional a manner. Someday,

Kyle was going to find something that made him look clumsy. Today was apparently not that day.

Kyle leaned up against the fridge, sipping his beer. "So, no girlfriend?" he asked as casually as his pounding heart allowed. *I'm not doing this. Damn it, I am not doing this. Dinner. With a friend. Stop it.*

"Not right now."

"Just say, *Kyle, shut up* if I get too personal, okay? Was there a recent one? Girlfriend?"

Peas went into the creamy orange stuff on the right back burner as Vikash either ignored him or delayed answering. "Last girlfriend was over a year ago."

"Oh. Sorry. Bad breakup?"

"Hand me that bowl. The green one. Thank you." Vikash managed to shrug and get orange-creamy stuff into the serving dish without spilling a drop. "It was civil."

"Of course it was. It was you. Was she—?"

"Kyle…"

"Got it." Kyle took the dish out to the table, already set for two. "Shutting up."

Even though the rooms were sparsely furnished and the kitchen was a sea of white, Vikash's apartment felt warm, the few things he did have tending toward cayenne and cinnamon tones, dark wood and brass. Vikash came out with two more bowls and a second trip produced *naan* and *raita*.

"Man, that all smells so good. I haven't had Indian food in forever."

"Some things you shouldn't deny yourself." Vikash pointed to each dish in turn as he took his seat. "Korma. Makhani. Curry. The Makhani's the spiciest. Extra veggies in everything."

"'Cause I don't eat enough of them." Kyle sat still when he spotted the puffball making cautious progress across the room. "I won't bite, Ellie. Promise."

The white fluff resolved into a cat with bright green eyes as she dashed from cover to cover, ever closer in her stealthy perusal of him. She was every bit as gorgeous as the fluffy white cat on the fancy kitty food commercial, her long white fur meticulously clean and tangle free. Kyle watched in amusement as Vikash set a small plate in front of the third chair at the table and tore a bit of bread into tiny pieces. She hopped onto the chair, still eyeing Kyle dubiously, and began to eat from the plate in dainty, polite bites.

"Doesn't she shed on everything?"

Vikash handed over the bowl of rice, indicating that Kyle needed to get with the program and start filling his plate. "I brush her. Twice a day. She's not allowed in my closet."

"She's beautiful. Persian?"

"Angora. Persians have smushed faces."

"Will she take something from me?"

Vikash's smile seemed more amused than usual. "Give her a pea. From your korma."

"Really? Cats don't eat peas," Kyle said on a snort even as he placed a pea on the china saucer.

Ellie sniffed the pea, ate it daintily, then stared right at him and mewed.

"Another?" Kyle carefully separated out another pea for her, which she promptly devoured. "You are quite the princess, aren't you?"

Vikash was watching Ellie, something odd lurking behind his eyes. "She belonged to one of my old boyfriends. He was going to open the door and let her go, so I claimed her."

Wait…what? "That's horrible. I hate people who think pets are disposable," Kyle spoke carefully since his brain had suddenly filled with sand. "Boyfriend?"

"Yes." Vikash didn't look away from the cat, a tiny hitch in his voice all Kyle needed to know on the subject.

"So you're bi." Kyle tilted his head to meet his partner's gaze. "Hey. Look at me. I think you know me enough by now. I'm not one of those people who have a problem with it."

Vikash nodded, though now his attention went to his food, that subtle shift in his shoulders letting Kyle know he wasn't happy.

"This is really good. All of it," Kyle said to fill the awkward silence. "Really, I'm impressed. I can't cook worth shit. I love this red one esp—"

"Kyle…"

He put his fork down, both palms flat on the table. "Look. Someone, maybe a lot of someones, weren't so nice about it. Maybe they were assholes about it. Do I look like them?"

"No." Vikash managed half of his serene statue smile. "You're too short."

"Damn right. Hey!" At least he'd gotten Vikash's smile to expand to a whole one.

"It's been a deal breaker. More than once."

"I'm not gonna say I understand." Kyle went back to eating so he wouldn't look like he was being confrontational. "Because I can't say that if I'm not you, right? But I'm not clueless. I hear the stupid shit people say. That no one's really bi. That you're just a greedy slut. That you're either really gay and in denial or really straight and playing around."

Vikash made a strangled sound that was definitely not a laugh, his eyes closed and his jaw too tight. *Nice, Kyle. You made it so much better.*

"Kash…I'm not one of those people. I don't think any of that crap."

Another nod, another tight smile, and Vikash went back to eating. A full five minutes went by before he murmured, "You gave me a nickname."

"Yeah. It kinda blurted out."

"It's fine. Certainly better than Kirby."

"Funny guy. But you don't call me that."

Vikash glanced up without raising his head. "I'm saving it. For when I really want to irritate you."

Kyle sputtered and huffed, then ruined the bluster with a huge grin. In that moment, an ice dam broke upstream and something warmer crept into Vikash's steady blue gaze. Through the remainder of dinner and second and third beers, Kyle learned more about Vikash than he had all week. In Vikash-esque fits and starts, with Kyle pulling and tugging like a world-class angler, he talked about his family — three sisters, two younger, cardiologist mom, professor dad. He admitted to a degree in music theory, explained his decision to attend the police academy as something more important than an academic life and mentioned the last boyfriend who had left him for not 'committing to being gay'.

Being fair-minded, Kyle offered as much as he received, without the extra prompting. He even scored one of those choking laughs when he told Vikash about his two much older brothers panicking when they found five-year-old Kyle on the floor amid the dogs, happily sharing their kibble.

"They were all set to call for an ambulance," Kyle said as he sat stone still to let Ellie sniff him. "When Mom came home, she couldn't stop laughing at them. It took her half an hour to calm Conner down and explain to him that it was gross, but wouldn't hurt me."

"You remember?"

"No." Kyle shook his head on a laugh. "But that's the kind of story that got repeated just about every holiday."

"Pictures?"

"No. At least not of that." Kyle finished his beer, the question of whether it was his third or fourth niggling at him. "Holy crow. It's later than I thought. Lemme help you clean up, at least, before I call it a night."

Vikash ruined the fluid rise from his chair with a tiny stagger. *Ha! I'm not the only one who lost track.* Whistling softly, ridiculously pleased with himself for all the breakthroughs that evening, Kyle snagged dishes and carefully avoided tripping over Ellie on his way to the kitchen.

"I think…" Vikash stared fixedly at the row of bottles on the counter. "The sofa pulls out. We're off tomorrow. I'd feel better if you stayed the night."

Kyle opened the door to the dishwasher, only half his attention on loading the dishes. "You know, you are a real mother hen sometimes. I'm fine and it's not like— Ow! Rotten fucking donkey balls!" He plucked the paring knife from the side of his hand where he'd managed to stab himself. "Teach me to look first."

"Let me see." Vikash reached for him, the little worry V between his eyebrows.

"I'm fine, damn it. Just stupid."

"Distracted, not stupid." Vikash grabbed his wrist, his grip gentle but his long fingers creating an unbreakable restraint. "Just…shh. Bleeding."

Before Kyle could struggle free or mount another protest, Vikash had his hand under the faucet, washing out the half-inch cut. He reached over and snagged a paper towel, gently dabbing at the blood.

"Am I gonna live, doc?" Kyle forced out as inappropriate, happy little fireflies zinged out through his body from the points where Vikash touched him.

"I think you might. Not as bad as I thought." His eyes widening, Vikash held Kyle's hand between them, drying it as carefully as he might have handled a baby mouse. He stopped suddenly and pressed the hand to his chest. "Kyle…"

"This…" Kyle swallowed hard, staring up into blue eyes that suddenly shone with a heart-rending vulnerability. "You know this is such a bad idea."

"I know. I'm sorry," Vikash whispered as he leaned closer.

"You should be. Getting a man drunk and taking advantage," Kyle murmured against soft lips suddenly pressed against his own. "Kash, I—"

Vikash stopped him by covering his mouth and pulling him close, his kiss as tentative and gentle as his hands. "Did I tell you I have a thing for gingers?"

"Green-eyed gingers?"

"Yeah."

"No." Kyle wrapped an arm around Vikash's back, stroking the hard muscles along his spine. *This is beyond stupid. I can't do this. Why can't I pull away?* "You didn't."

"Damn. Probably should have." Vikash released the hand he'd been clutching and cupped Kyle's face, his fingers stroking into Kyle's regulation-short hair. "Sorry."

"Of all the times for you to pick to talk too much," Kyle growled.

He gave up fighting the reins and let his body have what it wanted, surging forward to press Vikash against the counter, attacking his lips with ferocious need. Vikash's lips parted on a soft moan and Kyle seized the advantage, spearing his tongue inside that hot, spice-infused mouth. Arms tightened around Kyle, all of Vikash's careful, oversocialized behavior evaporated. He slid his hands down to cup Kyle's ass, his mouth answering with wild ferocity that shocked Kyle into a whimper.

Vikash broke the kiss, pulling back to search Kyle's face, his eyes dazed and glassy. "It's all right. It will be. We're attracted. We like each other. This doesn't have to be a big thing, right? Comfort. Between friends."

Friends? Okay, I can do friends. Better than a quickie we pretend didn't happen in the morning. Comfortable is good. "It's amazing none of your lovers ever killed you."

"Why?"

"'Cause you gab more during making out than you do when you're *supposed* to be talking."

Vikash smiled and put a finger to his lips. He disentangled partway from Kyle's embrace, closed the dishwasher then took Kyle's hand to tug him toward the back of the apartment.

The bedroom had more of an *I just moved here* vibe than the rest of the place. Pictures sat on the floor, presumably below their intended spots on the wall. Boxes still lined the space beside the closet. Nothing messy about it—no clothes lay strewn across the floor, no dirty dishes scattered about. It just felt unlived in, as if Vikash wasn't sure yet if he wanted to stay, or maybe he'd lost the desire to finish unpacking. Kyle found something achingly sad in the strictly regimented incompletion.

A queen-size sleigh bed dominated the center of the room, its head and footboard carved with vines. Neatly made with a burgundy duvet and ivory throw pillows, it was the only point in the room that felt permanent and stable. Kyle nudged Vikash backward until they stood beside the mattress. He had to rise up on his toes for a kiss, which he refused to be embarrassed about, as he started undoing the buttons of Vikash's chamois shirt.

Vikash had it easier and simply tugged Kyle's sweater up and over his head, but Kyle enjoyed the slow unwrapping, the pumpkin color of the material beautiful against Vikash's bronze skin. He uncovered a mostly hairless chest, natural, he believed, rather than waxed or some other nonsense. Long and lean, every part of Vikash fit that description. Nothing overworked or rigidly defined, just toned and gorgeous.

He slid the shirt down Vikash's arms, stopping to gape when he uncovered the gorgeous tattoo on Vikash's arm. Nine miniature dragons in flight, their bodies crossing and intertwining, decorated his skin from shoulder to elbow. One gold, two bronze, three brown, two green and one blue—something struck Kyle as significant about the number and colors. He traced the gold one's delicate head and it hit him.

"Fire lizards. You have Menolly's fire lizards on your arm."

"You read those books?"

"Damn straight." Kyle smiled as he traced the blue fire lizard's sleepy eye. "Loved Pern. Cried over some of those books, since I wanted my own dragon so bad."

Vikash nodded. "I wanted fire lizards. To sing with me."

"You play harp and stuff like Menolly?"

"Cello." Vikash leaned his cheek against the top of Kyle's head.

"You still play? Still have one?"

"It's…in storage." A distant chill colored those words.

Oh, damn. Hitting nerves again. Stupid. Stupid.

"You're furry," Vikash murmured as he slid a hand down Kyle's chest, apparently desperate to change the subject.

"Yeah. You okay with that? And I thought you were shutting up?"

In answer, Vikash leaned down to place a line of kisses along Kyle's collarbone, proceeding down over his right nipple to nuzzle at the forest of dark red hair in the center of his chest. Kyle thought his heart would stop when Vikash dropped to his knees and rested his head against Kyle's stomach with a soft sigh. It was too damn sweet.

"A fuzzy Kirby. Who knew?" Vikash nosed at the ginger line of fur leading down into Kyle's jeans.

Kyle tangled both hands in the thick black hair. "Really? Now you want to piss me off?"

"You're not. I can feel you laughing." Vikash kissed his stomach and sat back to undo Kyle's belt. "You're all right with this?"

"Whatever you're offering, I'm good with." Kyle curled forward for a soft kiss. "I trust you."

Those three words resonated through his bones. Yes. He did trust his partner, even though it hadn't even been a month. Vikash was a strange man with an odd sense of humor, but he'd been scrupulously honest. *And damn if he's not pushing all the right buttons here.*

Vikash popped the button and gazed up at Kyle as he took the zipper pull in his teeth. Perfect white teeth, of course. The heat in those blue eyes eclipsed all his doubts and Kyle stood frozen, entranced as the zipper descended one tooth at a time.

You're gorgeous. What can you possibly see in a scarred troll like me? But Vikash didn't pull away when Kyle's ugly hands stroked his face. He leaned into the touch and turned his head to kiss Kyle's palm. The jeans fell to the floor under the weight of keys and belt, and Kyle was abso-fucking-lutely glad that he'd managed to wear a decent pair of boxer briefs that day.

A sweet moan drifted up from Vikash as he hooked his fingers in the waistband and pulled the briefs down to midthigh. He buried his face in the thatch of hair surrounding Kyle's erection, nuzzling and breathing deep. His hands slid up the backs of Kyle's thighs to cup his ass, those long fingers just about covering his cheeks as he kneaded the tight muscles. Kyle kept his hold light on Vikash's head, stroking and urging but not demanding, not yet.

He hissed as Vikash ran his tongue up the underside of his cock, stopping to press against the bundle of nerves just under the head. "That's so good," Kyle moaned, struggling to keep still. "Damn. So freaking good."

He gripped Vikash's hair to guide his mouth, and that pushed some bells and whistles apparently, since Vikash immediately wrapped his lips around the head of Kyle's cock, a hard groan vibrating over the skin. Once he started, there was nothing hesitant or reserved about Vikash's approach. He swallowed Kyle down, sucking hard on each upstroke, tongue lashing at him mercilessly until Kyle thought he'd drown in sensual overload. With one hand gripping Kyle's hip hard, Vikash slid the other between Kyle's thighs to alternately pull at his sac and stroke his perineum.

Even though the hand on his hip was tight enough to bruise, Kyle rocked his hips, shoving him deeper. The heat, the obvious passion…and the fact that it had been a few months. Yeah. This wasn't going to be a marathon, maybe not even a five-k run.

"Kash...I'm..." The rush toward orgasm made it hard to breathe, his voice squeaking in mortifying ways. "I'm coming. Oh God, Kash!"

Vikash pulled off, pumping Kyle hard with his fist, closing his eyes and moaning as Kyle cried out and shot heated geysers all over Vikash's chest. Vikash turned them before Kyle's knees gave way and made certain Kyle was safely on the bed before he laid his head in Kyle's lap with a little sigh.

"That was hot," Vikash murmured against Kyle's thigh, squirming as he settled.

"Like barbecue-grill hot?"

"Like solar flare hot. I, um..."

"Did you?" Kyle struggled to sit up and pushed Vikash back. There was an undeniable spreading stain at the front of his jeans. "Well, look at that. You dirty boy. Guess we'd better get you in the shower."

It took a few minutes to get clothes untangled and to make it to the shower with all the groping and licking going on, but they managed without any disasters. They stayed under the hot spray long enough to both want a second round, jacking each other off while sustaining a lip-lock that threatened to drown them both.

Feeling suddenly shy, Kyle asked as he dried Vikash's back, "You still want me to sleep on the sofa?"

Vikash shot him a look that was hard to read. Wounded? Shocked? Harder still, since it only lasted an instant. "You're joking?"

"Just wanna be sure. Some guys like to sleep alone."

"Some guys are jerks."

Vikash put him in a playful headlock and dragged him to the bed. Tangled in those long arms, sinking into Vikash's wonderful mattress, Kyle slept better than he had in years.

Chapter Six

It should have been a full weekend off. With such a small precinct, every officer had to rotate on call for nights and weekends, so the rare whole weekend without even the one call at three in the morning to worry about? They were gems to be hoarded and relished.

Sunday morning, Kyle was wrapped once again in Vikash's arms, warm and well sated, looking forward to cooking eggs and vegetarian bacon for his partner. Ellie, who had warmed up to him enough to deign to sit in his lap for petting, slept at the foot of the bed. When both his and Vikash's cells rang, she catapulted from the bed and raced out with a hiss, tail bottlebrush-fluffed.

"Oh, holy fuck nuggets," Kyle growled as he dove for his jeans to yank out his phone.

Even though Vikash had been sound asleep half a second before, his fluid, serene movements got him to his phone first. "It's an alert. For us."

"I see it." Kyle plunked back against the pillows. There'd been a development in the Schuylkill murder case and the lieutenant needed them to come in 'sooner than possible' to talk to the officers on duty. "Fuck me. Why now?"

Vikash kissed the top of his head. "I can't fuck you right now. We have to get going."

"Hilarious. Damn it. I don't have a uniform here."

"I'll meet you there." Vikash retrieved Kyle's clothes from the floor and set everything neatly out on the bed. "Better if we get there separately."

Those words drove a spike through Kyle's chest. In their weekend idyll, pretending that the outside world didn't exist, he'd shoved the problems of sleeping with his partner aside. Of course they needed to arrive separately. Of course they needed to keep a professional distance on the job. He knew that, but somehow when Vikash said it so coolly, it hurt like hell. *I'm just warming a friend's bed. That's all this was. I'm not getting all maudlin and stupid about it.*

He yanked his jeans on, and the crew shirt he'd worn the day before, since he'd at least gone home Saturday morning and tossed some things in a bag. "All right, I'm out. Shouldn't hit traffic, so I'll see you in about thirty."

With his sneakers in one hand, phone and keys in the other, he was striding out of the bedroom when Vikash called, "Kyle?"

"Yeah?"

Vikash was staring at him when he turned, the carefully blank expression one Kyle was starting to recognize as distress. Maybe he'd had something he wanted to say, but all he managed was, "Don't forget your jacket's in the front closet."

"I got it. See you in a couple." Kyle hurried out with a feeling of lost opportunity and a lonely ache in his gut.

* * * *

When he got to the station, Vikash was waiting by the car with coffee, professional, calm, but the considerate gesture went a long way to soothing Kyle's hurt.

"A brown would've picked you," Vikash said as he handed over a cup and turned to walk beside Kyle.

"Usually, I can keep up with your thought jumping. But fuck if I know what you just said," Kyle muttered.

"If you'd impressed a dragon. It would've been brown," Vikash explained. "Not bronze, since they're strictly straight. And you're too tough for green."

Despite the residual tension in his gut, Kyle chuckled. "Gave this some thought, did you? But then you probably would, too, and that would be a problem."

Vikash shook his head and said far too seriously, "No. I'd have fire lizards."

"Right. Problem solved. I can't believe I'm having this conversation."

The building was quieter on a Sunday, so it was easier to hear conversation as they turned down the hall toward the squad room.

"No, it wasn't!" an angry young voice shouted. "I know what a fucking alligator looks like!"

Loveless' voice spoke over the young woman, authoritative and sharp. "It was dark. How could you be sure?"

"Carr, simmer," Zacchini said as she stood. "Monroe's here. Maybe it'll make sense to him." She hurried over to take Kyle and Vikash aside.

"So what've we got?" Kyle asked in an undertone.

"Me and Carr were patrolling along the river. Two kids out late along Boathouse Row. Something came out of the water and attacked them. Carr heard the screams, but by the time we got there, the animal—thing, whatever—was gone."

"Wait. Along the river? But we nabbed that guy. Is this something new?"

Carrington shook his head in obvious frustration and shooed Edgar away from his pen. "The lab report came back on your garden trowel this morning. The flakes were rust and dried clay. From what we've gathered, we're certain the incident last evening is connected where your cell phone thief was not."

"Ms. Yearwood here's fine." Amanda coaxed Edgar up onto her forearm and carried him back to his perch. "Her boyfriend's in the ER with a chomped foot. And Carr's probably not the best person for this."

This obviously meant questioning the witness, currently bristling and looking about two words short of punching Loveless in his condescending face.

Edgar paced back and forth on his perch, calling out, "Can't get it up! Can't get it up!"

"Edgar!" Carrington snapped. "Why can't you just say *nevermore* like a proper raven."

"Never say never! Never say die!" Edgar replied, hopping up and down until Amanda located his pens and placed them back in the cup on his perch. He was more than capable of retrieving his own pens when he dropped them, but he seemed to find it more interesting to take everyone else's.

"Looks like we're the cavalry." Kyle strode forward, hand held out. "Morning. I'm Officer Monroe. This is my partner, Officer Soren. We've been working on the attacks along the river. Loveless, you all right if we take Ms. Yearwood into the break room to ask her some questions?"

Kyle had to give the vampire credit. He put his obvious irritation aside to say, "Of course. Thank you for coming in."

The young woman, dressed all in black, shook Kyle's hand though her gaze traveled up and down Vikash. "Finally, someone nice."

Behind her, Loveless rolled his eyes, but thankfully stayed silent while Kyle led Ms. Yearwood out to the break room for a less formal conversation with coffee and snacks. Someone had left pizza in the fridge — Kyle's stomach reminded him he hadn't eaten. He sighed in disappointment when opening both boxes revealed pepperoni, but he brought them to the table.

Vikash peeked into the box. "Guess you can't just pick them off."

"No. Can't get all the residue off. Unless you want to call nine-one-one this morning."

"Not really." Vikash wandered to the vending machines and returned with a bag of trail mix that he placed in front of Kyle. "Just to hold you over."

"Thanks. Ms. Yearwood, do you have a first name?" Kyle asked as she raided the pizza box.

"Caitlin," she mumbled around the half slice she stuffed in her mouth. "God. Cold pizza in the morning is the best."

Vikash blinked at her and Kyle could only imagine what he was thinking about her table manners. He had to sip his coffee carefully so he wouldn't spray the table laughing.

"Glad you like it." Kyle leaned forward with his best *we're here to help* face. "Can you tell us what happened, Caitlin? Whatever you remember?"

Caitlin chewed for a moment, then said with her mouth still half full, "That other creep asked all this already."

"Sorry. I know. But if you could run through it for me and Officer Soren? So we can hear it firsthand?"

Vikash had his notebook and pen out, attentive and proper, and Caitlin addressed her statements to him. Maybe he looked like the more responsible partner. *Or maybe she's just eye fucking him... Stop that. He's gorgeous. Of course she wants to look.*

"Okay. So me and Colin, we were on our way home and he thought, hey, it's a nice night to walk by the river, with the moon out and all? He's kinda sappy that way, but whatever. We're walking by the boathouses and we get to a spot where a couple of the lights have burned out. And there's this splash. Like a big fish flopped out of the water or something, right?"

She stopped to shiver and took another bite of pizza. Kyle was starting to understand why poor Loveless had lost the little patience he had. "Did you look to see what the splash was?"

"Nah. River has stuff living in it. You don't think about it, right?"

"All right, so what happened next?"

"Okay, so Colin's talking about this new book he's reading, how it's all the best book ever and junk, and I'm all mm-hmm, and yeah, and not really listening. And this *thing* comes out of the water—"

"Pardon, sorry, were you closer to the water, or was Colin?" Vikash asked softly.

"God, you have the prettiest eyes," Caitlin said as she reached into the box for a second slice. "Colin—no, wait. I was at first."

Kyle took advantage of the break in her story. "And the thing? Could you see it? What did it look like?"

"It wasn't a freaking alligator. That's what it looked like," she said sullenly.

"Not an alligator is a little broad," Vikash said in his same even tone, but Kyle saw the little twitch of his eyebrow. "About how big would you estimate?"

"It was huge. Just…huge."

Kyle matched his voice to Vikash's, calm and reasonable, though he wanted to shake her. "Can you give us a comparison? As big as…"

"A taxicab. The monster was as big as a taxi."

"Good. That's a good start. Now I know it was dark, but what could you make out? Feet? Head?"

She finally abandoned the pizza. "It all happened so fast. It lunged at me. I screamed. Colin shoved me behind him, like he could do anything, the stupid jerk. And it bit him. Crunched right into his leg. He was screaming. I was screaming. I was holding on to him hard as I could 'cause that *thing* was trying to pull him into the river."

"All right. Deep breath. It must've been scary as hell. But anything you can remember about it might help. We can't let this thing run around loose. You say it bit Colin? So it had teeth?"

"No, it…it didn't. I don't know, maybe. But I didn't see teeth. It was more like…like a beak. Like a parrot has or something, right?"

Vikash's pen froze a moment at this surprising bit of information, but he picked right up again. Unflappable, was that the word?

"You're doing great, Caitlin. What else can you tell us?"

"It had these huge claws."

Now Vikash did stop writing, lifting his eyes without moving his head. "Do you remember seeing how many?"

"Four on each foot. These big, pizza-size feet."

Kyle exchanged a glance with his partner. He was sure Vikash didn't believe in coincidence any more than he did. "Anything else you remember? Anything at all. There's nothing we're going to think is silly or unimportant."

"You're gonna think this is stupid…"

"Whatever you remember. This thing tried to kill Colin. Anything you tell us might help."

"When Officer Stuckup came flying down the path with his partner and flashlights, the thing let go. I think the lights startled it or something. And it's sliding back into the water, right? And I couldn't help thinking it looked like that Godzilla movie monster."

"It looked like Godzilla?"

"No, like one of the other ones." She clicked her tongue in frustration. "And not, you know, Rodan. The one that looked like a turtle."

"Gamera?" Vikash supplied.

"Yeah! That's it! It looked like Gamera. Kind of."

After a few more questions, they left Caitlin with the pizza and Kyle pulled his partner back into the squad room where Loveless was drinking from an opaque, plastic-covered cup. Never a good thing to think too hard about what everyone knew was in there. Zacchini sat typing at her computer.

"Carr? Were you close enough to see much? Amanda?"

Loveless shook his head. "I saw something big sliding into the water. Couldn't make much out beyond size."

"I was a few yards behind. You know how fast Carr can move when it's dark." Zacchini shook her head. "What I saw afterward? Just murky impressions. Something big moving downriver underwater. It felt, I don't know, angry? What's that word that sounds like Maleficent, Carr?"

"Malevolent," Loveless said with a sigh.

"Yeah, that."

A clatter interrupted them, followed by Edgar screaming, "Go fuck a lamppost!"

"Shh, Edgar. You have five pens left. Chill. All right, I think we've gotten everything we could here. I want to go talk to the kid at St. Joseph's if we can," Kyle said as he made the wide berth around Amanda and Carrington to get to the front hall. "Sounds like you saved those kids, Carr. But maybe let Amanda wrap up for you."

"I've always liked you, Monroe," Zacchini said in her deadpan way. "Only man around here with sense."

"Don't leave me with her," Loveless groaned. "You see how she treats me?"

"Don't pretend she doesn't spoil you rotten," Kyle shot back. "Even I've been here long enough to see that."

"Tough love," Vikash patted the vampire's shoulder on his way out. "It's good for you."

Back in the squad car, back to Vikash being a silent ice sculpture, Kyle tried to keep his brain from spinning. He shouldn't read things into the silences, not when he'd gotten so accustomed to them before they'd slept together. He took them up Ridge Avenue and as they were passing the Fairmount Septa station, Vikash blinked rapidly as if he had been asleep.

"Snapping turtle."

"Spread it out for me, Kash. What did you just think of?"

"What Caitlin described sounds like a snapping turtle."

"Was it the Gamera thing?"

Vikash stretched, cracking his knuckles, and damn it, Kyle didn't need to think about those hands. "Partly. I grew up in Perry County. We had alligator snapping turtles. The beak. The claws."

"They usually get the size of taxis?"

"No." The word was short and clipped. Kyle braced for another flat tire, but Vikash went on. "Something in this city's making monsters."

Kyle chewed on his bottom lip before he answered. "Yeah. You're not the first to say that. There've been rumors. Things the top brass won't say. The real reason they put our unit together. I've tried to find things out. Looked into other cities' paranormal units. No one seems to have the kind of cases we do. Nothing like this."

"Kyle…"

"Yeah?"

"Would you think less of me if I said I was a little scared?"

Kyle patted his partner's knee. "I'd think less of you if you tried to pretend you weren't. This is some pretty scary shit."

"More or less scary than Lime Jell-O monster?"

"I'll let you know when we catch sight of this thing."

The kid at the hospital, Colin, didn't have much to add to Caitlin's statement. He echoed the sighting of beak and claws, and added that the thing definitely had a shell, adding fuel to Vikash's giant snapping turtle theory. That and the fact that his leg wound matched the shape of the ones on the two homicide victims. Beyond that, the poor kid was drifting on pain meds while the surgeons tried to decide if they could save his leg.

"I don't suppose anyone's going to see this as an Animal Control issue," Kyle muttered on the way out of Emergency.

"Doubtful."

"Two dead, one badly injured, and a monster that uses the Schuylkill as his hideout and personal rapid transit. What the hell are we supposed to do here?"

"Put everything in front of the lieutenant."

"Without a plan of action? Without anything concrete beyond *we think it's a giant fucking turtle*? Seriously?"

"It's her job. To make decisions."

Kyle turned in alarm at the frost in Vikash's voice. Invisible electric spiders raced up his spine. "Kash…don't…not here."

Vikash closed his eyes, a muscle jumping in his jaw, but the tingling didn't fade. Desperate, Kyle grabbed his arm to shake him and gasped as the tingling became an electric storm raging through his veins. The world tilted underneath him as the electrical surge echoed inside him. He had no other word for it as he clutched at Vikash's shoulder, trying to stay on his feet.

"Kash," he whispered, and there might have been a whimper, his, Vikash's. Someone was dragging him down the sidewalk. A sudden turn, an alley with Dumpsters.

Vikash, it was Vikash still beside him. The lean muscles under Kyle's hands tensed and Vikash let out a sharp cry as if he flung an angry verbal spear into that alley. The charge in Kyle's body ripped from him, directed by that resonant cry. One of the Dumpsters shuddered, rumbling a few inches across the ground. Then its lid flew back, its contents exploding to send trash raining down in sodden, squelching clumps. The metal sides of the Dumpster had buckled outward, sharp, twisted bits of metal protruding in unruly patterns.

If Vikash hadn't flung an arm around him, Kyle would have dropped to the ground, his sight wavering in and out. He heard Vikash talking to someone, explaining about a possible pipe bomb, and he realized he was sitting in a chair back in the ER's waiting room.

"Kyle." Vikash crouched in front of him, forehead crinkled, eyes just a little too wide. "Hey. Talk to me. Please. Kyle?"

"I'm... I think I'm okay. Definitely in what-the-fuck mode. But stuff is staying still now."

"Good. The uniforms from the 22nd are investigating the, ah, explosion. They're done with us. Think you can get to the car?"

With Vikash hovering, Kyle managed to stand and even walk with credible steadiness, though his legs felt like pudding. He wasn't tracking reliably, not quite yet, since Vikash asked him several times for the keys before he managed to fish them out of his pocket.

"Station?"

"Just to return the squad car. I'm taking you home."

Kyle put his head back and closed his eyes. "So assertive and shit. I'll be fine. We need to talk about what happened back there."

"I'm not sure," Vikash whispered.

"Right. This is why we talk about it." Kyle slumped in the passenger seat. *Nauseous. Still woozy. Definitely not okay yet.* "Let's review. I get pissy and say stupid shit. You get mad. Your thing-in-which-bad-things-happen starts to wind itself up. I grab you, and my weird thing, which should suck your thing up... Okay, that didn't come out right, but you know what I mean. And it kinda does. I feel something. But it's like the something is bouncing around inside me."

"It echoed," Vikash still whispered, his distress practically fogging the windows. "You grabbed me and it echoed back and forth between us. It...grew. I don't know how else to describe it. I was scared it would hurt someone. Lots of people. I didn't mean to get so angry."

"Kash, look at me. Don't turn the car on yet. You can't drive like this. Look at me." Kyle waited until those blue pools of anguish turned to him. "You directed it. I felt you do that. You sent the thing, the power, the energy in a direction *you* chose. Do you usually do that?"

"No."

"Didn't think so." Kyle let his eyes drift shut again. "Damn it. For everyone else, I'm Kirby. For you, I'm a fucking transformer."

The strangled laugh was unexpected, so Kyle cracked an eye open. "What?"

"Sorry." Vikash gave him a strained smile. "Just picturing you turning into a VW."

"Aw, man, really? You turn me into an Autobot and I have to be Bumblebee? This is another short joke, isn't it? One of these days, you're really gonna hurt my feelings with those."

The strangled sound turned into a choking one. Alarmed, Kyle sat up, only to find Vikash with his head on the steering wheel breathless in the throes of his version of laughter.

"I mean, I know you wouldn't let me be Prime, but I could at least be Ironhide or Sideswipe or someone cool." Kyle snorted. "Bumblebee."

Vikash wiped at his eyes with a last snicker. "I'm glad you're okay."

"Great. I'd be better if you'd acknowledge my badassness." Kyle subsided to take stock of how bad it was, decided he wasn't going to puke in the car, and let Vikash pull out onto the street in peace. "We have a ton of crap to lay out for the lieutenant tomorrow."

"Yes."

Simple as that, no gloating, no need to rub it in that he was right. "You really could try a little harder. It's so hard to hate you sometimes."

* * * *

After a bit more patient argument, Vikash ended up staying the night at Kyle's place. He could grab a few things and come back in half an hour, he had insisted, but he refused to leave Kyle alone for longer than that.

"You were white and shaking," Vikash finally admitted softly. "I thought you were having a seizure."

While Kyle wanted to be annoyed at the hovering, he felt too much guilty pleasure at having an extra night with Vikash wrapped around him. There were so many ways for this to end badly. He just wasn't ready to face reality yet, and he got the morning that had been stolen from him the previous day with him cooking breakfast and Vikash lounging at the table in a bathrobe. It was way too fucking early a morning, since Vikash had to dash home before work and feed Ellie, but Kyle was firmly entrenched in *I'll take what I can get* mode.

When they caught up to each other at the station later, even morning roll call was easier with Vikash there. Kyle took an end chair, and Vikash sat ramrod straight beside him, a barrier against all comers. Instead of isolating them, though, Kyle's fellow officers had become more relaxed around him and actually greeted him in the morning, chatting and joking. Sure, they kept a prudent distance, but the ritual of *oh my God, there's Kyle, where can I sit that's safe?* That no longer happened.

Vikash hung back when roll call was over, and though Kyle was eager to get things going that morning, he stayed, curious as to what his partner was thinking.

"I know what some of us do," Vikash said when everyone else was gone. "But not everyone."

"Um, okay? What's this about?"

"We need to trap the snapping turtle."

"Right. We talked about that. And?"

Vikash leaned a shoulder against the wall. "It'll help me think this through."

"All right." Kyle sat nearby, turned to face his partner. He still felt ungodly tired. "You know about Gatling and Virago. And Loveless, more or less."

"I know Carrington's a vampire and he faints in full sun. No vampire superpowers?"

Kyle snickered. "Poor Carr. Good thing he's not here for that assessment. He does better in the dark. Great night vision. Scary fast. Stronger than human. No turning into bats or mist, though."

"All right. Wolf? Is he a werewolf? Does he even have a first name?"

"Um, no. To both." Kyle hesitated. He'd never figured out if Wolf was delusional or the stuff of fantasy novels. "He claims that he *is* a wolf. That some curse or spell turned him into a human. Trapped him in a stupid human body, he says. I'm not sure it's true. But he's stronger than even Carr is at night. Super good hearing and sense of smell, so *something's* going on with him."

"Krisk?"

"Your guess is as good as mine. No one talks about Krisk. He just…is."

Vikash blinked, his only show of surprise, before he went on with his interrogation. "Greg Santos?"

"Please don't laugh."

Now Vikash's eyebrow shot up. "I'll try not to."

"Greg hears the unhappiness of waterfowl."

"Don't even know what to say to that."

"Most people don't." Kyle held up his hands. "Don't get me wrong. He's a good cop."

"Amanda? I know she has visions. But of what?"

"Ha. Well, Amanda calls herself a site-specific post-cog."

Vikash shook his head slowly. "I obviously haven't had enough coffee yet."

"It's like being a precognitive, but she only sees visions of things that have already happened relative to the spot she's standing in. On. Around. You know what I mean."

"That must be…confusing."

"She says she's used to it. Like having a heads-up display on a dashboard."

The questions stopped, Vikash's eyes glazing over, and Kyle knew enough to leave him alone while he processed. Finally, he twitched and came back. "One more. Virago's problem. Can he *expand* flame in humidity even if he can't call it?"

"Don't know. Not asking him. He really can't stand me, Kash."

"Any idea why?"

"Maybe he's a bitter closet case? Maybe because I've gotten him chewed out a couple times? He hates redheads? He's jealous 'cause I'm better looking? Hell if I know."

Vikash's smile warmed Kyle from the heart out, the subtle heat in it just for him, a secret intimacy where they couldn't acknowledge more. "I'll ask Jeff."

An unusual sight greeted them as they left the meeting room. The badass leather jacket, flanked by Virago and Gatling, was floating down the hall toward the front door. In the set of its shoulders and the swinging of its arms, it managed to look smug.

"Cutting him loose?" Kyle asked in surprise.

Gatling answered before a red-faced Virago could launch into a tirade, "Yeah. We were holding him until the state paranormal unit could pick him up. But DA said we can't hold him. Jacket has a lawyer. Who knew?"

Vikash strode in front of them, forcing them to stop, but his objective wasn't to prevent the jacket's leaving. He offered his hand. "Be careful out there and try to stay out of trouble, Mr. Jacket."

The jacket made a gesture with one sleeve as if it were crossing its heart. Then it held out the sleeve and met Vikash's hand in an approximation of a handshake. Kyle walked away, shaking his head, while Vikash stayed to speak to Jeff.

An odd air of anticipation hummed through the squad room that morning, laughs just a bit high-pitched, conversations just a bit hurried. Everyone knew the nature of the river monster by now and waited to hear what would happen. An itch lodged between Kyle's shoulder blades as several sets of eyes tracked his progress across the room to the lieutenant's office, where Vikash caught up to him again.

"Don't stand there looking spooked, Monroe," Lieutenant Dunfee called from her desk. "Get in here and shut the door."

She waited, dark fingers drumming on her desk until they'd settled. "I hear we have a suspect. Of sorts."

"Yes, ma'am." Kyle cleared his throat. "Of the nonhuman variety."

Vikash pulled the photograph of the clawed footprint from the file he'd brought in and let Kyle do the explaining, walking through the steps that led them to believe their murderer was a giant snapping turtle.

"Probably immune to bullets, too," the lieutenant said with a sigh. "All right, gentlemen. You look like you have more for me. Spit it out."

In fits and starts, Kyle explained about the intersection of his and Vikash's dubious psychic talents while she leaned back, lips pursed.

"I knew there was a reason I put you two together. But this wasn't what I had in mind," she said when he had finished. "Could this happen accidentally? This combination of destructive weirdness?"

Vikash shifted in his chair, obviously uncomfortable. "I don't...think so, ma'am. Kyle has to be close or in physical contact. If we keep some distance when I'm angry, it won't happen. I'm not an angry person. Very often."

"Comforting. Though in the week you've been here, we've had three separate incidents."

"I've been a bit on edge, ma'am. This isn't the easiest precinct to transfer into."

She leaned forward, her expression more sympathetic. "No. I'd imagine not. Was this just a heads-up for me, or are you two leading up to something? Which, if that's the case, spit it the hell out."

"Yes, ma'am." Kyle wanted to put a hand on Vikash's shoulder, to take his hand, anything to wipe away that half-guilty, unhappy look in his eyes. Since he couldn't do that, he settled for taking the burden of conversation. "We'd like to propose a sting operation of sorts. Something to draw the turtle monster out so it can be apprehended."

"You mean you want to set someone up as bait," she countered in a dry tone.

Impossible to argue that. "Um. Yes. There doesn't seem to be a pattern in its choice of victims. One male, one female, one couple. But all late at night, on the weekend for whatever bizarre reason, and they all were walking on the Waterworks side of the river, all between Boathouse Row and Spring Garden Street."

"What I'm struggling with is why this creature doesn't eat its victims," she said, her eyes narrowing. "Why would it take people from the bank, kill them and put them back?"

Vikash cleared his throat softly. "Something that Zacchini said. She said it felt malevolent."

"Wonderful. You think this thing is killing for fun?"

"Yes, ma'am." Vikash nodded. "It fits the facts."

"In this department, we have muscle, early-warning systems and even fire power..." Kyle hesitated here until Vikash gave him a little nod. "Between Soren and Virago. Different kinds of firepower, but enough that I think we could split the department into two teams and get this thing off the street. Er, river."

She fixed them with a level stare for so long Kyle was certain they were about to be tossed out on their ears. "All right. We have a few days. I want this written up, this operation you're proposing, Monroe. Have it on my desk this afternoon, and I'll run it by the powers that be. I'll let you know."

"Ma'am, if I—"

"Out. I have a sacrifice coming up. You don't want to be here."

On that dire warning, Kyle hustled Vikash out of her office, his partner craning his neck to watch her shut her door and pull the heavy black curtains over her windows.

"Kyle?"

"It's okay. I mean, it is if she does these on schedule. Lieutenant Dunfee is the anti-priestess of an elder god. As I understand it, she has to perform certain rituals to keep the god from manifesting, which would be A Very Bad Thing."

Vikash sank into his chair at their shared desk slowly.

"You all right?"

"More or less." Vikash pulled up a document template and started typing. "I was a normal cop about a month ago. With as normal a life as a cop can have. Pardon the delayed shellshock."

"I'm sorry. It kinda hits at unexpected moments. You want me to give you a few minutes?"

"Unexpected moments," Vikash muttered. "Ancient evil god and it's an *unexpected moment*."

"Sorry." Kyle gestured toward the break room. "Maybe I'll just, um, wander away for a minute? Get you something from the machines?"

"Sit down, Monroe." Vikash's voice didn't change in inflection or tone, but a little tremor ran through his hands as he typed. "We have work to do."

Translation – I'm trying not to freak out. You abandon me now and my head will explode. "See Kyle sit." He plunked down and pulled up his system. "Sit, Kyle, sit."

"I didn't mean it that way."

"I know. S'okay. My snark is on automatic sometimes."

The next few hours were spent quietly texting back and forth across the desk as they formulated a battle plan.

Chapter Seven

Wednesday, with their proposed plan of attack submitted and no new cases on their desks, Vikash suggested a walkthrough of the area around the last attack. They parked in the lot by the Waterworks and began a stroll down Boathouse Row. The timid breeze wasn't enough to cut through sun-warmed clothes, and Kyle had to fight to keep his mind on business since their reconnaissance felt more like a date than police work.

Even if Kash would take his hand in public, Kyle wasn't stupid enough to try it on duty. Still, it was a nice scenario. The two of them out on a day off, just wandering together, stopping for lunch. Maybe a little making out on a secluded bench. Kash sent the fantasy scattering by making it clear his thoughts were all business.

"Fences. Can it climb?"

A bit of a smug, satisfied warmth nestled in Kyle's chest that he was beginning to follow his partner's mental leaps. "Maybe. But if our witnesses are right about the size, something that heavy should be bending chain-link fencing if it goes over. I'm not seeing any of that."

"No." After they walked past several more clubs, Vikash continued. "The non-fenced ones."

"Probably. Think we should check for turtle prints? Maybe this thing has regular spots where it likes to come ashore?"

They'd finally reached Sedgely Club, the beautiful boathouse on the far end with its big bow window and its lighthouse, when Kash finally answered. "Turtle Rock."

Kyle shook his head sideways as if he had water in his ear. "Nope. Sorry. You lost me."

With one hand, Vikash traced the outline of the lighthouse in the air. "The Light on Turtle Rock. Don't they call it that?"

"Oh. Yeah. They do."

One corner of Vikash's mouth tipped up and damn it, Kyle wanted to kiss him there, on that half a smile. "Oddly appropriate."

"Heh. Guess it is."

A goofy smile of his own threatened and Kyle chewed on his bottom lip to keep it at bay. The way Kash's mind continually spun in silence amazed him, impressed him, sometimes even intimidated him a little. It was a gorgeous thing, to watch the process, and being able to without distractions on a sunny, quiet morning made him want more private hours than he had a right to. Dinners out, drinks after work — they didn't have to call it dating, right? What would it hurt?

"Hey, Kash, what would you say to —"

Vikash cut Kyle off by smacking the back of his hand against Kyle's biceps and pointing toward an isolated car parked farther down along the river trail. A figure moved furtively beside the car, using a flat piece of metal to try to jimmy the door open. Kyle squinted at the bit of black leather he could make out.

"Oh, hell no. Really?"

"Are we stepping on toes?" Kash asked, already moving forward with purpose.

"Since this is Carr and Amanda's beat? None of us care about that."

"Good."

Kyle had to jog to keep up with his partner's long strides, and Vikash did *stride*, his jaw clamped so tight, Kyle worried those perfect white teeth might crack. It shocked him into missing a step when Vikash called out, "Mr. Jacket!"

The second shock of the day came when the leather jacket startled, dropped his impromptu tool, and instead of speeding away, hurtled toward them. Kyle's hand went for his nightstick, but Vikash's hand on his arm stopped him, and his partner's instincts were better than his. Leather Jacket glided to a stop in front of them, gesturing frantically with one sleeve toward the car he'd been trying to break into.

"Guess we better take a look," Kyle said as the jacket used the opening of his cuff as a sort of hand and began tugging on Vikash's sleeve. "Maybe there's a baby in there or something."

"Is there a baby?" Vikash asked as the jacket dragged him along, but Leather Jacket twisted his upper half in an approximation of a headshake.

When they reached the car, Leather Jacket pointed with his sleeve, knocking against the back window with the buckle on his cuff. Vikash leaned over his shoulder to check the back seat while Kyle went to the other side.

"No baby. Or puppy," Vikash announced, and though the back seat was trashed, the mess couldn't have hidden an infant, human or canine.

Leather Jacket threw up both arms in an obvious gesture of exasperation and pointed again.

"There's… It looks like a pile of baggies under the front seat," Kyle said, squirming around to block the sun's glare and get a better look. "Maybe, just could be—"

"White powder. Yes," Vikash finished for him. He took Leather Jacket by the cuff and tugged him gently over to a nearby bench where he sat on one side of the jacket and Kyle took the other, with Leather Jacket perched on the wood slats on his bottom hem in his approximation of sitting.

Kyle let out a slow breath. "So were you after the drugs in the car? To take them?"

Leather Jacket crossed one arm rapidly over the other in a negative gesture.

"Ah." Vikash stared at the car, then turned to the jacket. "Were you trying to implicate the owner of the car?"

After a hesitation, Leather Jacket did his odd bending nod.

"For revenge?" Kyle asked softly and got another negative arm wave.

"I think he was trying to help," Vikash suggested. "Trying to catch one of the bad guys."

The nodding was more emphatic this time, and Kyle slid down farther on the bench with a sigh.

"Appreciate that you want to. Really, it's commendable. But if we broke into that car, and the stuff under the seat was, oh, talcum powder or icing sugar or something, then we would've just done something illegal."

"Even if they are bags of drugs," Vikash added gently. "We don't have any reason to search that car. It's illegal search and seizure, and the criminal walks away. Even if you know the person who owns the car and you know those are drugs for sale on the street, we'd still need a warrant. You'd have to be able to give a convincing statement for a judge to approve it."

Arms folded across its, or perhaps *his* front, Leather Jacket nodded slowly.

"We appreciate that you want to help, Mr. Jacket." Kyle nearly reached over to pat the jacket's knee before he recalled there was no knee to pat. "And you can, but you have to do it the right way. You can tell us when you've seen something. Be our —" He was about to say *eyes and ears*, but choked off the words, wondering if that was offensive as well as inaccurate. "Witness out here. Let us know when you see something bad happening."

Kyle got the weirdest impression that Leather Jacket was side-eyeing him. One sleeve came up to where a human ear would have been, the jacket wriggling back and forth and gesticulating with the other sleeve.

"We know you can't call us," Vikash said, obviously better at speaking jacketese, and now that Kyle knew what the gestures meant, damn it if the jacket hadn't managed sarcasm. "But you could meet us. Here. Wednesdays?"

Leather Jacket did his version of a nod again. No smartass undertones for Vikash, of course.

"Speaking of seeing stuff," Kyle said with a nudge to the jacket's side. "Seen any giant turtles around lately? Say, the size of a car?"

The body of the jacket reared back and a visible shiver ran from collar to the ends of the cuffs. Leather Jacket turned to Kyle then Vikash before nodding slowly.

Vikash patted the sleeve nearest him. "Did it attack you?"

Using his cuffs, Leather Jacket spread his plackets apart to show the empty space within.

"Oh." Kyle thought he had it. "No meat to chomp on?"

"And no interest in good leather, I suppose," Vikash added, leaning back against the bench. "The monster turtle has no taste."

This time when Leather Jacket shook, it was a whole jacket, rhythmic shaking while he rocked back and forth. Mr. Jacket was laughing and somehow it made him less of an oddity, less of a monster — more relatable, if not exactly human.

"Can you show us where you saw it?"

The answer was a vague wave toward the river, followed by swimming motions with his sleeves.

"Swimming," Vikash confirmed. "Did it come ashore?"

Leather Jacket pointed to the side of the Sedgely Club opposite the lighthouse where the beautifully kept lawn unobstructed by shrubs ran down toward the river. Kyle did a quick walk through while Vikash 'talked' to the jacket, an odd minuet of half sentences and expressive gestures. If the monster had left prints, they'd been washed away or obscured by greenery, so Turtle Rock didn't seem to be a regular landing place. *Good to know*.

Kyle mentally filed that away, though Vikash probably had detailed notes, and they said goodbye to Mr. Jacket. He seemed to have promised, at least according to Vikash, not to engage in any more vigilante activity. The rest of the day ambled quietly by, strangely peaceful both out in the streets and back in the squad room. Despite the general air of calm, Kyle discovered that he'd lost every ounce of courage he'd ever possessed.

He shook out his damp palms while Vikash started packing up for the day. "Hey, um, Kash?"

"Hmm?" Vikash's attention was on his backpack as he fished out his keys.

"You..." Kyle's voice actually cracked. This was ridiculous. He'd already slept with this man, knew how much Vikash wanted him, and here he was waffling, afraid of a change of heart, a change of mind, a careful reconsideration after a couple of days in the harsh daylight. "Wanna stop over my place for a beer? I've got, um, all the extended Lord of the Rings movies?"

"Geeks," Amanda muttered on her way out.

"But they're our geeks," Carrington admonished as he jogged to catch up with her. "Do you have time to look at my car, Manda?"

They breezed past, oblivious to the churning in Kyle's stomach and the odd look Vikash was giving him.

"Ellie's expecting me," Vikash said quietly.

"Yeah, um, she's a cat. How would she know if you're a little late?"

Vikash gave him an almost smile. "She knows. Bring the movie. And the beer."

"To your place?" *Damn it, stop squeaking*. "Oh, sure. Great. See you in a bit."

With a mock salute, Vikash left as well, leaving Kyle to try to locate his jumping heart before he followed. *He said yes. He said to come over. What's wrong with you?* The fact that Vikash had neatly sidestepped following Kyle home shouldn't have mattered. It didn't really. "He's just cautious. Not a big deal," Kyle muttered as he shut down his system.

What was he trying for here, anyway? A little house in the suburbs with a picket fence? A puppy? Not that

Ellie would probably allow a puppy, but Kyle put his desperation to call this a relationship down to being alone so long. He had a good partner now. They got along and that they so far got along in bed too was just a bonus. He wasn't going to push and ruin a good thing. What he did manage to do, instead of staring at his desk as if zombies had made his brain into an afternoon snack, was to get his ass home, get changed into civvies and drive to Vikash's place.

"This should be easier this time, right?" Kyle parked and banged his head against the steering wheel a couple of times, just to see if he could knock anything loose, or back in place, or whatever the hell was wrong with his head. "Idiot. Going up there. Having a beer with a friend. If something happens, it happens. If it never happens again, you're gonna have to deal."

That right there was the problem, wasn't it? Now that he'd had Vikash's hands on him, had kissed him, had watched that gorgeous face while Kyle made him come, there was no way Kyle would ever get him out of his system.

"And now you're staring at the door. Good, Monroe. Doing great." Kyle shook his head and pushed the buzzer beside that cheery red door.

This time Vikash seemed a little out of breath when he opened the door, not quite askew exactly, but was his hair still wet. He'd showered? "Hi."

Kyle held up the six-pack carton. "Beer. Hop Devil. And movie, as commanded."

"Suggested." White teeth made an appearance in Vikash's smile. "Come on up."

The warm welcome and the sight of Vikash in jeans and a blood-red, body-hugging Henley pummeled some of Kyle's nerves into submission as he trudged up the stairs behind his host. Either that, or his brain simply shut down.

"Snacks? Did you eat?" Vikash asked as he went straight to the kitchen.

"Um…" Kyle stopped in the living room to let Ellie sniff his shoes. He obviously met some standard since she didn't run and hide this time. "No?"

Vikash *tsked* as he started pulling things out of the fridge — several bright blue bowls, a platter of artfully arranged things Kyle couldn't make out from across the room. He wasn't sure if he should be annoyed that Vikash had assumed he'd forget to eat or gratified that his partner already understood him so well.

"Out," Vikash murmured as he took the beer and shooed Kyle toward the couch. "Before you hurt yourself."

"Hey! I'm not incompetent in the kitchen."

"You impaled yourself loading the dishwasher."

"Never gonna live that down, am I?"

"No."

Kyle contented himself with getting the DVD set up. He did feel like a bad guest, though, as Vikash strode back and forth from the kitchen with opened beers, a tray of cheese and olives, hummus and pita chips, and a blue bowl of something that smelled incredible, which he plunked down in front of Kyle.

"Dinner." Vikash took the remote from him and sank gracefully onto the other end of the sofa. "Eat that first."

"Okay, Mom," Kyle grumbled, but he picked up the bowl and nearly drooled over it as he breathed in the steam. Vegetarian chili. The first bite had him moaning like a grizzly hunkered over a salmon at the cumin-chili-jalapeno goodness. "Damn."

"Good?"

"Hot, but yes. *Where have you been all my life* good."

Vikash snorted and popped a dark olive into his mouth. "Shh. Starting. Love the beginning."

"Sorry," Kyle whispered as Cate Blanchett's liquid velvet voice started the introductory voiceover. He snuggled back into the couch cushions, wolfing down his chili, and felt *happy*. He'd seen the movie a hundred times, but watching it with Kash felt new, and the space between them on the sofa no longer felt strained and artificial. No way he could explain it, but this was comfortable.

Didn't hurt that every time Vikash reached for something from the miniature feast on the coffee table, he edged closer to Kyle's side of the sofa. By the time the unscheduled fireworks went off at Bilbo's birthday party, Vikash had encroached far enough for their knees to touch. When the hobbits were about to be attacked on Weathertop, Vikash settled an arm on the couch behind Kyle.

"Oldest player cliché in the book, Soren," Kyle murmured and snagged several slices of cheese as the Nazgûl on screen closed in.

"Don't want you to be scared." Vikash nestled closer so their thighs pressed against each other. "There's a players' book?"

"Shh. Nazgûl."

Kyle would never admit it, but this part of the movie did freak him out a little. The warmth beside him and Vikash's arm stealing more firmly around his shoulders both served to stave off the shivers he usually got during this scene. Once, on a dark night filled with thunder and whipping rain, he'd even fast-forwarded through it. Not that he would ever admit that out loud, or the fact that he'd checked the locks several times before going to bed.

By the time Arwen began her desperate race to Rivendell, Vikash was definitely nuzzling at Kyle's throat while Kyle pretended to ignore him.

"You know it wasn't Arwen in the book, right?" Kyle asked to see if Vikash was still aware of the movie in even a peripheral way.

"Mmm." Vikash nibbled on his earlobe. "Glorfindel. I like that they gave her a bigger part. Made her a person."

"Oh, yeah. Not gonna argue there." Kyle devoured one more bite of pita and hummus before he turned to drape his legs over Vikash's. "Damn it. Amanda's right."

Vikash lifted his head and blinked. "Oh?"

"We're so, so geeky."

With a soft chuckle, Vikash leaned over to suck a leftover bit of hummus from Kyle's thumb and he couldn't have stopped the moan even if he'd stuffed a sock in his mouth. "Kash…"

"Stop?"

"Not…necessarily. But the movie?"

"Leave it," Vikash murmured against Kyle's jaw.

"Oh, yeah. Okay. 'Cause we can probably both recite it anyway and it's kinda cool background noise with the music and all. I love this soundtrack—"

Vikash cut him off by sucking on Kyle's bottom lip, turning the rest of his sentence into a garbled moan. Careful of the dishes on the coffee table, he turned to stretch out on his back and Vikash obliged by adjusting in controlled graceful movements until he hovered over Kyle, knees on either side of his hips.

"Kash?" One hand combing through the thick ebony of Vikash's hair, Kyle locked eyes with him. "You have something in mind?"

"It's not obvious?" Vikash's arms tensed around Kyle and his words sounded strangled.

"Well, yeah. But we never talked about any of this. What you like. What you don't like."

Vikash rested his head on Kyle's shoulder with a long release of breath. "All right. You start."

"Me? Oh, I'm easy. So long as I get to come, right? Top, bottom, everything in between. Not into pain, thanks. And I won't call you Daddy."

The choked sound was probably a snicker and not a muffled sob—at least Kyle hoped so—but when Vikash raised his head again, those blue eyes were stone serious. "I'd never hurt you. Not on purpose. And I'll settle for you calling me Your Majesty."

Kyle smacked him with one of the fussy red-orange throw pillows. "You pick the weirdest times for jokes."

"It's fine. Whatever you want. I haven't…bottomed often." One black eyebrow twitched on the last words.

"We never have to if you don't want. Ever."

Vikash kissed his nose. "Didn't enjoy it then, but I was young. We were young."

"Ah, young and stupid and thinking you knew everything. Been there." Kyle slid his hands under the hem of Vikash's shirt to stroke up either side of his spine, the skin warm and smooth. "You'll tell me if you want to someday, and we'll do it right, okay?"

"Mmm." Vikash eased a knee between Kyle's thighs. "Don't want any of that tonight."

"No?" Kyle let one of his legs drop over the side of the couch so Vikash could settle between. "Why not?"

"Condoms are in the bedroom," Vikash whispered as he licked a heated line down Kyle's throat.

Kyle yanked the shirt up and forced Vikash to stop treating him like a lollipop so he could pull his head and arms out. "Got it. It's laziness."

Long, nimble fingers had undone the buttons of Kyle's shirt before Vikash answered. "I don't want to let go of you right now. Not even for that long."

What the hell am I supposed to say to that? "I have that effect on people."

Despite stupid shit popping out of Kyle's mouth at the worst times, Vikash didn't get up and leave. He chuckled and curled over to suck on Kyle's collarbone, causing him to arch up and let out an embarrassing mewling sound.

Kyle slid his hands down to cup Vikash's beautiful ass, kneading taut muscles as Vikash moved over him, unbuttoning his jeans. It took a bit of wriggling, twisting and a good bit of snickering before they were both naked, but then Kyle took Vikash by the arms to keep him still.

"Gorgeous. You know that, right?"

The sound Vikash made could have been equal parts agreement and dismissal, but trying to parse his partner's various grunts faded from his list of important things to think about when Vikash's lips closed hard over Kyle's nipple. A ragged moan escaped—his, Vikash's, maybe both of them giving voice to their desperate need in tandem.

Vikash lifted his head, concern lurking behind the fog of lust in his eyes. "You don't think the thing will ever happen during…?"

"Our amplification echo chamber of doom during sex?" Kyle arched up, trying for some friction on his aching cock while Vikash held himself up out of reach. "You planning on having angry sex?"

That beautiful white smile pierced right through Kyle's core. "No."

"Good. I mean if we ever do, we should make sure we're outside somewhere. Where there's not so much stuff to break. But not really my thing, usually."

Whatever anxieties Vikash had latched on to obviously had ceased growling at him and had curled up in the corner. He lowered his body onto Kyle's, the furnace heat enveloping him. He gasped as their cocks brushed, then aligned, lying side by side in eager anticipation. So simple, so uncomplicated, this brush of skin on skin, and the rush of sensation still threatened to overwhelm him.

"Kash," Kyle whispered against Vikash's shoulder, but it wasn't a question or prelude to an objection. Affirmation, breathless acknowledgment of this sparking, crackling connection, and Kyle clutched tighter, shoving his hips up as much as Vikash's weight allowed.

Vikash hooked a hand under Kyle's knee and pulled, dragging his leg up, letting out a soft, plaintive sound when Kyle's heel brushed over his ass. He might be all aloof composure in public, but Mr. Marble Expression wanted someone to hold him. Tight. Kyle was more than happy to oblige by wrapping both legs around Vikash's waist and locking ankles at the base of his spine. A deep moan rewarded him as he tightened his grip with all four limbs, the reverberation rumbling down into his bones, Vikash rocking against him in a slow, sensual slide.

"Hey. Over here."

Vikash lifted his head from where he'd been nuzzling Kyle's throat. His blue eyes, so shockingly beautiful against his tawny skin, crinkled at the corners when he smiled, an expression that nearly stopped Kyle's heart. *Oh, you've got it bad, Monroe. Fell down the rabbit hole when you weren't even looking, didn't you?*

When Vikash lowered his mouth to Kyle's, there was no zip of electricity like you read about in love stories, no psychic bond formed because Kyle just realized how deep his heart has decided to plummet into this. But Vikash's lips were soft, firm, gently exploring his in a way that was both insistent and tender, and Kyle did feel like he could melt into a puddle on the sofa cushions. He wrapped his fingers tightly in Vikash's hair and pushed forward, tongue insisting on entry until Vikash opened his mouth with a hard moan.

Somewhere in the distance, Gandalf led a mixed species crew of brave adventurers over the Pass of Caradhras while fell and terrible things tried to throw them from the mountainside. It all faded into background noise behind Vikash's poignant, soft sounds of pleasure and his panting breaths through that magnificent nose.

The slide of body against body ratcheted up from sensual to heated, from heated to frantic.

Kyle broke the kiss first, teeth clenched in frustration. "Kash…I need…"

While it wouldn't have taken a genius to figure out what he needed, he was still grateful that Vikash was quicker than most. He leveled himself up on one arm to give himself room and wrapped his free hand around their dueling erections. Enough pre-cum had leaked from both of them to provide a bit of slick and Vikash rolled both foreskins back and forth as he began to pump. The strong grip around Kyle's cock had him bucking under Vikash, his overloaded nerves almost sending him screaming.

"Are you…?"

"Close? Oh, hell yes." Kyle hissed through his teeth as Vikash tightened his grip and started pumping faster. "Damn it, Kash, just a little, just…"

"Faster? Harder?" Vikash panted out.

"Yes. Everything, oh *holy fuck*," Kyle cried out as the tightening in his balls reached overwound spring state, his orgasm hitting like a two-by-four between the eyes. He was sure the neighbors heard him bellowing, maybe more of a banshee shriek than a manly bellow, but he really didn't care.

Vikash's strokes reached frantic as he raced to join Kyle, his own sounds softer, but somehow more desperate in their strangled, dearly bought lower volume. Heavy ropes of spunk splashed Kyle's chest, warm and sticky and smelling of brine and male and *Kash*. Sure, Kyle might have whimpered a couple of times, too sensitive in the aftershocks with Vikash still touching him, stroking him. He wasn't so macho that he'd deny it.

And Vikash? He had the damn nerve to snicker.

"What the hell is so funny?"

"I was just thinking," Vikash panted out. He sat back on his heels as Kyle lowered his legs, tracing lazy designs in the cum on Kyle's chest.

"Yeah? What were you thinking?"

"I was thinking." Vikash stopped to make that choked laugh sound again. "You weren't terribly quiet. What if the neighbors called the police?"

"Okay, fine. That's kinda funny."

Kyle held out his arms and let Vikash fall into them, surprised that he allowed it because of all the sticky. For a few moments, well into the scenes in Moria on the television, Vikash still snickered. Kyle contented himself with holding Vikash close and stroking his hair until he'd calmed down from whatever weird fit of nerves or relief or whatever it was he was having.

"We should probably clean up and stuff." Kyle hated be the one to say it, but if he got too comfortable, he'd fall asleep. If he fell asleep, he'd have to rush back home in the morning since he still didn't have a spare anything at Vikash's.

When he reached for the remote, though, Vikash caught his arm. "Not yet. Movie's not over." He nestled in more comfortably, reached over Kyle to pull the coffee table closer with its food and laid his head on Kyle's shoulder. "Just stay. Please?"

He stayed. With his heart fighting between expanding with joy and cracking from grief, because this was getting to be a worse idea all the time for him, he stayed and tried not to think about previous relationships his boyfriends didn't want publicly acknowledged, or how bad an idea it was to get involved with your partner no matter what the circumstances.

Kyle pulled the blanket off the back of the couch and settled it over both of them, an unsettled feeling in the pit of his stomach as they watched Gandalf fall to his Balrog-induced death.

Chapter Eight

Late Saturday night, every officer attached to the 77th was at the station house in street clothes, including Krisk, who apparently had civilian clothes tailored to accommodate his tail. The deep brown of his sweater actually looked good with his greenish skin.

"Who knew Krisk had taste?" Loveless muttered to Zacchini.

"Who knew he had street clothes?" Zacchini responded.

Lieutenant Dunfee strode out of her office and clapped her hands together once, the sharp sound silencing conversation. "Ladies and gentlemen, what we're asking you to do tonight wasn't in anyone's original job description. We understand that. The objective is to contain and capture. If you find you're unable to do this safely and your team is forced to put the beast down, no one will fault you. If you find yourself or your teammates in jeopardy and you must withdraw, no one will fault you. What I do expect is that you'll put your egos aside and work together.

Watch out for each other. Protect each other. Every officer comes back, understood?"

Murmurs of "yes, ma'am" ran around the room.

"Monroe and Soren, Zacchini and Loveless are with you. Lourdes, Santos, you're with Gatling and Virago. Wolf and Krisk, I want you as close to halfway between teams as you can manage. Whichever team makes contact, that's where you go. Teams will coordinate with me. Keep channels open. Clear?"

Nods and verbal acknowledgment from the officers joined with Edgar screaming above the door lintel, "Fuck him up! Fuck him up!"

Squad cars were to stay at the station that evening. Kyle's team all piled into the lieutenant's van and she would drop them just north of the boathouses. The other team would start at the south end of the target area.

"You're bait, Monroe," Zacchini said from her place in the second row seats.

"Me? Why me?"

"Because Carr's gonna smell weird to it. Vikash is almost a foot taller than any of the victims."

"And you?"

Zacchini shrugged. "You just look more attackable. Seriously. Carr, if you were gonna pick a victim, who would you go after?"

"Oh, Kyle, definitely," Loveless drawled from where he sprawled in the corner. "He's just so nice and compact."

"Oh, for fuck's sake. Everyone wants to take a crack at the short jokes these days. I'm average. The Internet says so."

"Of the four of us, you're the closest to the profile," Vikash said reasonably.

"Great. You can call my mom and tell her I was turtle food."

"You could just absorb it," Loveless said with an airy wave.

"Doesn't work like that, Carr."

Vikash nudged him. "We'll be right there with the net."

The Kyle-as-bait thing wasn't a shock. He'd talked about it with Vikash earlier in the week and he was griping out of habit and nerves. Hell yes, the whole thing unnerved him.

"It won't get a chance," Vikash whispered to him. "I won't let it."

Kyle couldn't help a little smile in the darkness of the back seat. No officer wanted to see one of their own go down, but he had more than that. Someone was fiercely concerned just for him.

Lieutenant Dunfee pulled over on Kelly Drive near the end of the boathouses and turned in her seat. "Last chance to back out, Monroe."

"I got this, ma'am. I mean, they've probably got Lourdes playing bait on the other end and the monster'll come after her first. And then get the shock of its nasty life when cars and Dumpsters start smashing into it."

There were a few grim chuckles as the team piled out. Lieutenant Dunfee had her finger pressed to her earpiece. She spoke a few words, glanced up, and jerked her head at Kyle. "They're in position. Go."

Kyle gave a jaunty salute and sauntered off down the river trail. A shiver made him hunch and shake his shoulders out as he passed the Sedgely Club. The trail was well-lit here and the lighthouse cast its beacon out onto the water, but he couldn't help recalling the badass leather jacket's sighting of the monster. Maybe he hurried past a little faster than he should have for someone who was supposed to be putting out a strolling, come-and-attack-me vibe, but he did breathe a little easier and slowed his steps when he cleared the Sedgely's well-kept and river-exposed lawn.

After the Sedgely, he didn't expect anything to happen this far up where the boathouses sat closer together. The Snapping Turtle of Doom would have a far better opportunity later again. He'd worn white sneakers and a white T-shirt under his much-faded jean jacket, all the better for predators of any sort to spot him. There were a few people out, couples walking close, a few loners walking quickly, but for the most part, the river walk wasn't as well-lit or as populated as he would have liked.

I hope I don't get mugged before the damn thing shows up.

He had the ridiculous urge to rush back and give Vikash a kiss, like some hero going off to battle, but he managed to restrain himself. Really, he needed to have a talk with his brain about agreeing with his baser urges too often. He'd bring pie charts and graphs to the meeting and be terribly stern.

Instead, he gave his partner a thumbs-up and meandered downriver along the trail. *Just a late-night stroll. Taking in the moonlight. Got no place to rush off to.*

Past the tidy stone and red tile building for the Philadelphia Girls Rowing Club, past the Undine Barge Club that had always reminded Kyle of a medieval castle, past the smaller, more practical Penn AC and College Rowing buildings.

As he approached the Vespers Boat Club, he tensed. The Tudor-style building with its turrets and balcony railings cast odd shadows in the moonlight. The trees overhung the trail here, blocking out much of the light, and Kyle strained for the sound of a splash over the crunch of his steps through fallen leaves. There was a broad stretch of lawn between Vespers and Lloyd Hall with no fencing between the water and the river trail. The perfect place for a snapping turtle ambush.

I hate this. God, I hope the damn thing is down by the Waterworks. But no splash sounded, as Caitlin had described. Kyle was almost past the open lawn, almost to the relative safety of Lloyd Hall, when a hiss and a rustling came from the right.

"Shit!" Kyle yelped and leaped back as a huge beaked head lifted from the shadows beside the trail to snap at him. "Fuck, oh, fuck!"

He backpedaled toward the street, the monster coming after him much faster than stumpy-clawed legs should have allowed. A smaller shadow flashed by him, heading toward the monster. Carrington flung himself between Kyle and the snapping beak, and tossed one end of the net over the monster's head. The mesh caught and the vampire yanked hard, trying to pull the massive head around and away from Kyle.

"Grab an end!" Carrington yelled. "We have to get the rest of the beast tangled in the net!"

Kyle was already diving for the trailing end of the net, pulling it out and over the turtle's back where it managed to get one foreclaw tangled in mesh. Running footsteps pounded down the path, Amanda and Vikash catching up to them.

We're gonna do this. It's going to be okay.

Just as this premature triumphant thought crossed Kyle's brain, everything went to hell. There wasn't even a handbasket in which to toss the pieces. The monster reared up, as no turtle should, ever, and pulled Carrington off his feet. It jerked its head, flinging him so that he flew several yards through the air. Now there was a splash, though only indirectly caused by the turtle.

"Carr!" Amanda dropped her part of the net and raced toward the water.

"Damn it, Zacchini! We need you here!" Kyle shouted, but she didn't slow down.

"He can't swim!" she threw back over her shoulder, no hesitation in her steps as she waded out toward the frantic splashing where, presumably, their vampire was busy drowning.

The momentary distraction cost Kyle. He caught the movement too late as the monster surged toward him. It lifted a foot and knocked him down as if he weighed no more than a plastic bowling pin. Its claws gouged into his side and thigh, pain blinding him as it began to drag him toward the river. Before it got far, strong hands hooked under his shoulders, trying keep him onshore, Vikash swearing softly beside his ear as the tug of war quickly became one-sided.

"No! You can't have Kyle!" Vikash shouted. Were there tears in his voice? No, that couldn't be. "No!"

The electric sparks of Vikash's anger popped and spat along Kyle's spine, so intense that the agony of sharp claws anchored in his flesh faded into the background. Kyle tried to relax, to let it flow through him as Vikash's conduit and amplifier, hoping the explosion of anger would save him.

The damn monster had other ideas.

Just as Vikash's power was gathering for a strike, several things happened that never should have in any universe. The snapping turtle's giant beak chomped through the mesh. Its head shot forward to fasten on Vikash's shoulder. Even as Vikash screamed, something flew out of the dark to beat at the massive turtle head above them, leather sleeves slapping hard at amphibian skin.

The badass leather jacket had dashed to Vikash's rescue.

A ground-rattling roar ripped from the monster's throat. It hurled the jacket and Vikash away just as Vikash fired his blast of psychic fury. The thud of Vikash hitting the side of Lloyd Hall coincided with a crackling bang that reminded Kyle of an M-80 going off in a metal trashcan.

The massive shell cracked in several places, liquid oozing through the gaps. The leg pinning Kyle exploded outward in a rain of gore and bone. With a gurgling groan, the mighty Snapping Turtle of Doom collapsed on the grass, twitching.

"Aw, man," Kyle whispered, swallowing bile. He crawled out from under the remains of the foot and dragged himself over the lawn to Vikash. Blood trickled down his side, though it was hard to say how much was his and how much was turtle explosion.

"Kash? Give me something here. You alive?"

Nothing. Kyle reached him on all fours, dragging his injured leg. "Come on, Soren. Don't feel so good. You're not a very considerate magic thrower, you know. Making your human wand feel like crap. Lemme know you're okay before I pass out."

White teeth flashed in Vikash's smile, though that might have been pain instead of humor. "On your knees for me, Sweet."

Kyle struggled out of the ruins of his jacket to ball it up and place it under Vikash's head. "Can we concentrate on the important things here? Like how bad you're hurt?"

"Not sure. Shoulder's either popped out or broken. Head's swimming." Vikash gripped his arm, maybe to make certain he was there or to keep the world still. "How's Mr. Jacket?"

The leather jacket lay inert beside Vikash, acting inanimate, as a leather jacket should. "It doesn't look good."

"And the monster?"

"Er." Kyle lay down beside Vikash because he couldn't sit up anymore. "You appear to have blown it up from the inside out."

"Oh. Gross." In the silence, they could hear Carrington coughing up a lung and possibly throwing up whatever quantity of the Schuylkill he had swallowed. "Sorry about that. I just wanted to get it away from you. Not kill it."

"Don't think this was something the state paranormal unit could keep in a tank, Kash."

Wolf's voice came from somewhere nearby. Probably up on the trail. He was calling for ambulances. Good thinking. There should be several. Maybe an air evacuation.

"Jacket tried to save you," Kyle muttered.

"Don't let them…leave him here."

Him? Sure. Why not? Kyle reached over Vikash and pulled the leather jacket close. "Got him. Kash?"

"Hmm."

"You're scary when you get mad."

"Told you."

Sirens wailed and howled in the distance. Ambulances. Squad cars.

"There's mud in my ear," Carrington's shaky complaint reached them from the riverbank. "How is there *mud* in my *ear*?"

Everything would be fine. Normal was already reasserting itself. Scary how a half-drowned vampire cop complaining about being dirty had become normal these days.

* * * *

The hospital flicked by in a mess of disjointed images for several hours as Kyle faded in and out. The too-familiar utilitarian crush of emergency registered at some point, then an X-ray tech explaining something he couldn't follow. Doctors hovered. Nurses moved him. Eventually, he caught up to the world's rotation again and had a lucid moment in a quiet, semi-private room.

A slender nurse with short black hair smiled at him when he focused on her. "I'm putting your jacket in the closet, Officer Monroe. Such a nice leather jacket."

"Rrmph." Kyle's first try at speech was a little rusty. He cleared his throat. "Thank you?"

Oh, right. Mr. Jacket. Good. He made it here.

He blinked at the curtain drawn through the center of the room as he tried to find the right button to elevate the head of his bed. "How long am I stuck here, ma'am?"

"At least through tomorrow for observation. You lost too much blood and the doctors want to watch for infection."

Kyle did his best to be patient through IVs and doctors poking and prodding. At least Vikash came to see him, his arm in a sling, and his serene smile back in place.

Amanda came to collect him when they discharged him two days later, with news that Vikash was resting at home and Carrington was back at work. She helped him gather his things together, her solid, stoic presence a comfort and a tolerable substitute for who Kyle really wanted there.

"Ready?" She held a hand out to help him into the waiting wheelchair.

"Oh! We can't forget Mr. Jacket! He's in the closet over there."

But when Amanda opened the little closet's metal door, the hangers were empty.

* * * *

Kyle lay on the cinnamon-colored sofa with Vikash reclining against his chest as he flipped through the five hundred channels of Saturday night TV wasteland. Maybe it wasn't entirely comfortable, but Vikash's arm was still in a sling so they couldn't reverse positions.

He'd come out of nearly being a toy for an evil monster turtle pretty well. The gash on his hip was the deepest, but no organs were punctured, no bones broken. Vikash had the nasty bite on his left shoulder, still healing, and while the right arm hadn't broken, it had popped out of the socket and torn muscle along the way.

Kyle missed being able to see the whole fire lizard tattoo, but he was a patient man. It would be there when they had both healed.

"We could watch wrestling," he suggested.

"No."

"How about this reality show about—"

"Kill me now. If you have any pity."

Kyle chuckled, stroking Vikash's hair. "You know I'm kidding. Why don't you have Netflix on this thing?"

"Just haven't yet." Vikash gave a one-shouldered shrug.

"Not even YouTube. You really don't have this set up for anything, do you?"

"Not yet."

"I could always—"

"Kyle. Stop."

Kyle sighed and turned off the TV. The giant plaid elephants in the room were starting to make a nuisance of themselves and it was making him antsy. Since coming home from the hospital, Vikash had withdrawn more and more into his silences again. While he had a suspicion what caused some of it, Kyle could only guess. He was tired of guessing.

"Hey." He wrapped an arm around Vikash, careful of the sling. "You're worried. I can tell you're worried. Is it about us being partners? With the amplification and the explody stuff?"

"No. Not really." Vikash sat up and move to the opposite end of the sofa. "It can't happen accidentally."

"Guess not. Takes a lot of effort. You think we need to practice? Get better at it?"

"Something to consider." Vikash looked away and the increasing distance between them was killing Kyle. It *felt* like a spear through his chest anyway.

"Is it about Leather Jacket? We did the best we could. Not our fault no one can find him."

Vikash shook his head, all his concentration apparently on combing the fringe on a throw pillow.

"Kash, damn it. Shit eats at you from the inside long enough, you're gonna be the one that explodes."

"I was just thinking."

"Were you? I've never seen you do that." Kyle ducked the pillow tossed at his head. "What about?"

Even with the pillow assault, Vikash wouldn't look at him. "It just… I really like you. More than anyone in…a while."

"Okay. I like you, too. Kinda nice to like your partner."

Vikash nodded and finally lifted his head. "That's just it, though. If you weren't my partner, I could ask you out. We could…date. Not worry about people seeing us together too much."

"Got it. And, yeah, I get it." Kyle ran both hands through his hair, not quite mussable since he kept it so short. Vikash's need to keep any hint of a relationship hidden was frustrating, but he got it. In most departments, it was heavily discouraged or completely forbidden. "Let's take it one thing at a time, okay? Not get ahead of ourselves. We get along great. We're good working together. And sleeping together."

"No fraternizing policies?"

"Are bendable in this weird unit you've landed in. Look, it's not like either one of us is gonna engage in massive, embarrassing PDAs at work, right? And it's not like we're even moving in together or anything. Mia Dunfee isn't going to kick either one of us off the force just because we share a bed sometimes. Hell, Lourdes and Santos do it and no one says a thing."

Vikash blinked. "They do?"

"Yeah. They do. They're a weird couple, but everyone knows they've been together almost since they met. There's only so many of us. Lieutenant knows that. So long as it doesn't cause a problem at work, she'll pretend not to see."

"And if it does? If we can't do both?"

"Both what? Work and sleep together? She'll probably try and reshuffle partners first, for the good of the precinct."

Vikash had edged closer to him again, the frost melting away. "Who could she put you with? Safely?"

"Well, not Virago. That would be bad for so many reasons. Not least of which is he can't stand me. And Jeff's about the only person who puts up with him. And you can't break up Wolf and Krisk. Who else understands Krisk?"

"She'd have to put you with Carrington and me with Amanda."

"What? Oh, hell, no. I am not playing vampire herd. Freaking high maintenance, overeducated…" Kyle trailed off when Vikash's lips curved into a statue smile. "You're messing with me."

"Maybe."

Kyle opened his arms and let Vikash settle against his chest again. "Jerk."

One thing at a time. What else could they do? Maybe they would talk about having a drawer and closet space in each other's apartments soon. Maybe someday they would talk about moving in together, or at least meet each other's families. Kyle's mom would adore Vikash and he'd be good with taking him over there tomorrow. But they both had to be ready. For now, Vikash felt good in his arms, a good puzzle-piece fit, not the kind you had to take a hammer to. He felt better than he had in a long time and with Vikash, he could face any weirdness yet to come.

THE PILL BUGS
OF TIME

Dedication

For everyone who has ever felt that his or her talents don't quite fit. It's a wide, weird universe and we need one of everything.

Chapter One

Normal was something one left at the door when assigned to a paranormal police station. Officer Vikash Soren had seen that demonstrated the first time he had set foot inside the 77th. During roll call, the man who would later become his partner had accidentally shot fire from his fingers at the ceiling. Someone else's fire, as it turned out. In the weeks that followed, he had encountered an animated leather jacket, worked with a vampire, a lizard man and various officers of dubious paranormal talents, and had helped stop the killing spree of an alligator snapping turtle the size of a sedan.

It would follow that nothing should surprise him anymore.

But when he walked into the squad room that morning, late due to a doctor's appointment, his colleagues had gathered around the periphery of the room to watch Greg Santos in a fistfight with a puddle of water.

Coffee cup in hand, he wandered over to lean against the desk beside his partner.

"Hey, Kash." Kyle gave him a quick glance, his attention fastened on the unlikely pugilists. "Everything go okay?"

"Yes. Shoulder's fine."

"You're not even going to ask, are you?"

Vikash sipped his whipped cream-drowned mocha latte. "You'll tell me."

"You saying I talk too much, Soren?" Kyle nudged him with an elbow. "One of us has to. The suspect was originally an ice tree. Tree-ish. Thing. It was ice and looked like a three-year-old had built a tree out of Legos."

Carrington Loveless III, the department's nutritionally challenged vampire, came to lean against the desk on Vikash's other side. "It was, as I understand it, standing on the Ben Franklin Parkway and hitting people as they walked by. Didn't seem to be causing injury, but we can't have an ice beast swatting tourists' asses. Harassment, at the very least. Bad for the city's image."

"It melted?"

"Why, yes. Yes, it did." Carrington's smile was just half a fang short of evil. "Melted through the net in which Santos had snared it, and the resulting puddle goosed him. Things escalated rather quickly from there."

Greg didn't seem to be making any headway, other than getting soaked. "Should get an Odo bucket," Vikash murmured.

"A what?"

Kyle chuckled into his coffee. "Seriously, Carr? You never watched *Deep Space Nine*? The character who could only retain a solid shape for so long?"

Carrington sniffed. "Masters level courses in geek. Between the two of you, that's what I'd need to decipher half your conversations."

"This from someone who sings opera in the car," Carrington's partner, Amanda Zacchini, muttered as she walked past, her steps hindered by the piece of equipment she carried. Shira Lourdes, Greg's partner, hurried after her with an armful of some sort of corrugated hose.

"I like a lot of music!"

"Moody, dark, emo music, sure," Amanda countered, though her attention was on what she and Shira had brought in, most likely from Amanda's truck, since they'd tracked in snow as well.

When Amanda attached the hose, Vikash finally recognized it — a Shop-Vac, of the sort people had in their garages or by their workbenches. He shook his head as he hurried over to get the vac plugged in for Amanda. While the male squad members had been standing around watching the struggle, some of them taking bets, their two female members had been deriving a solution.

Without another word, Amanda switched on the vac, sucked up the water combatant, removed the hose and jammed a rubber ball in the opening, effectively trapping the animated water and leaving Greg panting on the floor.

Lieutenant Dunfee had just emerged from her office, eyebrows raised. "Do I want to know?"

Perched on top of the lieutenant's doorframe, a bright-blue and neon-pink bundle of feathers flapped its wings and let out a raucous croaking laugh. Edgar, the department's foul-mouthed raven, finally decided to weigh in. "Water sports!" he called out. "Not safe for work! Fucking amateurs!"

Lieutenant Dunfee shot him a withering glare. "Enough with the editorial, Edgar. What the hell is going on out here?"

"Under control, ma'am," Amanda deadpanned. "But I'm filing an expense report for a Shop-Vac. Just so you know."

"Get it on my desk. I'll sign it. See what the bean counters make of *that*." The lieutenant pinned Greg with a hard stare. "Santos? You need medical assistance?"

Greg climbed to his feet hastily, wiping the back of one hand across his split lip. "No, ma'am."

"Good to hear. Back to work, ladies and gentlemen. Try to keep the violent confrontations to a minimum today."

A rather disgruntled and damp Greg Santos stalked off to the men's room to clean up while Shira continued with booking the combative puddle.

"Just another day," Vikash murmured as he finally took his seat at the desk he shared with Kyle.

"Hmm?" Kyle glanced up from his typing. "Oh. Yeah. Though I'm thankful for any day free of explosions and imminent death. Or are you having a paranormal existential crisis again?"

"An amused one."

"Well, damn. If it'd been the other kind, I could get us takeout from My Thai, light some candles and put on *Princess Bride* when we got home."

"Kyle. Work." Vikash said it gently, but it was all he could do to keep his gaze from darting about to see if anyone had heard.

"It's not like I'm yelling," Kyle hissed. "God's sake, Kash. The paranoia's getting a little old."

"Work is work and home is home."

"Yeah, yeah, and never the twain shall meet. It's not like I'm cornering you for a quickie in the conference room. Or locking lips over lunch."

"Interesting development."

"What?"

"The increased alliteration when you're upset."

"I'm not *upset*. Just a little irritated that you keep jumping and twitching if I get too close anywhere outside one of our apartments. We're both professional at work. I don't insist we hold hands those rare times we go *out* to dinner. Ticks me off that you keep acting, I don't know, *embarrassed* about us."

"You promised to stick to professional at work."

"Easy, Soren." Carrington patted his shoulder as he strolled past. "Suggesting takeout for dinner is hardly unprofessional."

"You heard?" Vikash's heart thudded against his breastbone. *The whole department knows. Everyone can see.*

"Vampire ears, my dear. What don't I hear? Seriously, though, relax. No one has time to care about your little illicit tryst."

Vikash might have taken the advice if Virago hadn't bellowed across the room, "Hey! What're you girls whispering about? Going to some rainbow and glitter bar?"

"Only if you come with us!" Kyle made kissy face noises in Virago's direction. "Don't forget your purse!"

"Shut it, Vance," Amanda muttered as she stalked past and smacked Virago on the back of the head. "Your conf…confucking…what's the word, Carr?"

"Conflation," Carrington called back without missing a beat.

"Yeah, that word…of gay men with actual chicks is offensive."

"Sorry, Manda."

Normally, Vance Virago, self-proclaimed tough guy, cringing as he apologized would have been amusing. Vance couldn't have heard them from across the room. He was merely bullying Kyle as he always did. But the timing was horrible, and between those homophobic words and Vikash's twitching, they had managed to erase the contented ease from Kyle's face. It gutted him that Vance could do that. Worse still, Vikash had no idea what to do about it.

"Kyle…"

He didn't have a chance for even a minimalistic explanation or apology though, since an alert popped up onscreen from the lieutenant, ordering them to a disturbance in Fairmount Park.

Vance shoved violently back from his desk. "Aw, man!"

And our resident homophobe is our backup. Irritation crawled up Vikash's spine. Kyle had never done anything to Vance except refuse to crumple under his bullying. Some days it was bad enough that Vikash wanted to file harassment charges on Kyle's behalf, though Kyle would resent the interference. Still, it was wrong and— *Oh, damn.*

Through his rising anger, Vikash felt the uncomfortable heated ball of power at his core heralding his strange talent manifesting. He nearly panicked, the urge to reach across the desk and grab Kyle overwhelming. Together, they had a chance to direct the lightning blast of anger somewhere harmless. Maybe the old paper shredder that jammed after every page. But touching Kyle also meant the power would amplify in some bizarre melding of their broken paranormal talents. Not to mention, touching Kyle in the squad room just gave Vance more ammunition.

Then it was too late for choices. The power surged from him as he sat stone still, fighting to keep any reaction from his expression. A pop and a distinct electronic sizzle sounded on his left and he cringed.

"Fuck me!" Vance shouted, batting at his smoking computer monitor.

Jeff stood to help him smother the tiny flames with a towel. "Damn it, Vance. What did you do now?"

"I didn't do it! I swear!"

"Lieutenant's gonna stop letting you have computers if you keep breaking them."

Vikash turned back to find Kyle staring at him instead of watching the commotion, his lips clamped together in an angry line.

"I don't need you to protect me, Kash."

"It wasn't…it got away from me."

Kyle snorted. "Obviously."

Tamping down a sigh, Vikash grabbed his hat and followed Kyle out to their squad car — white with the blue blaze like all Philadelphia city police cars. Their department had the black and gold 77th shield over the blue stripe as well, though, forever branding them as something different.

For once, Vikash wished the ride to a scene were longer. Not for the first time, he wished he could be light on his verbal feet. "Kyle…"

"Put it all somewhere safe for me, Kash." Kyle reached over to pat his knee. "Hold on to whatever's percolating and baking in there. Right now, we've got two phrases we need to worry about. *Disturbance* and *attacked by a ball of sticks.* Let's not lose focus when we don't know what the fuck we're walking into."

"As usual."

"Yep. I love surprises."

"You hate them."

"Shh. I'm trying for a bit of self-delusion here. Don't spoil it for me."

There it was again. Despite all his guilt and doubt, Kyle had bent the wire hanger of his words, jimmied his way in and hooked a smile from Vikash. Sometimes, like now, a little burr of irritation went with the smile — that Kyle could make him lose even that speck of control. But it still wrapped a layer of warmth around his battered heart. Kyle was like a blanket straight from the dryer on a winter morning. The rather sappy image made Vikash snicker.

"What?"

"Nothing. Blankets. And dryers."

"You are *so* freaking weird some days." Kyle nodded to their onboard computer. "Please tell me we have an update on the last location. Saying *in Fairmount Park* is as bad as saying *somewhere between here and Lancaster*."

"Mount Pleasant."

"Thank you, gods of specific landmarks."

Vikash turned his head as a street sign flashed by. "The GPS says to take Kelly Drive."

"The G-freaking-PS can go fuck itself quietly in the corner. I've lived here all my life, Kash. Reservoir's gonna get us there faster."

"The GPS isn't really designed for that."

Kyle flashed him one of those beautiful, crooked grins Vikash adored so much. "Probably not. But it could have a lot of fun trying."

Four inches of snow had fallen the night before, coating the browns and greens of the park in a uniform layer of white, softening the aggressive lines of statue plinths, hiding the imperfections that the spring thaw would reveal in shameless stripper fashion. Bright winter sun plucked golden sparks in Kyle's red hair. Kyle Monroe, with his once-broken nose and his burn-scarred hands, who couldn't have been more beautiful to Vikash if angels had burnished his skin.

I'm in love with him. I'm in love with my partner and I can't tell him. Don't dare tell him.

For Kyle, being with a man wasn't a big deal. Nothing relationship-wise seemed to be with him. As far as Vikash could tell, Kyle had never had a serious, long-term boyfriend. While Vikash? He had always struggled — to explain to his family that he was bi, to re-explain that fact constantly to every significant other he ever had, to hide who he was at work with meticulous care. Bad enough to be a gay cop, but an out bisexual cop? It would be like tossing a chocolate unicorn in a locked room full of starved squirrels. Picked apart bit by bit until there was nothing but crumbs.

Every time his reserve, his well-hidden anxiety, his inability to *pick a side* — as his last girlfriend had put it — had scuttled his relationships. They had seen it as a lack of commitment, as if his bisexuality were an automatic gateway to infidelity and promiscuity. Kyle wasn't asking him to change. Kyle at least said he understood, but the restlessness had begun, the irritation with the fact that he simply couldn't be open and out in public, that he had to keep work and home life in hermetically sealed boxes. It wouldn't be long now before Kyle reached his limit.

Vikash had insisted they each keep their own apartments. He insisted they come to work separately. He was the one who twitched away when Kyle tried to take his hand across a restaurant table. Self-sabotage? Probably. He was good at that. Though this time it was a choice he didn't want to make between relationship and career, and the longer he avoided facing that choice, the more he guaranteed spectacular and messy relationship failure.

When Kyle turned onto the normally peaceful, tree-lined avenue of Mount Pleasant Drive, there couldn't be any doubt they were heading in the right direction. Small clusters of screaming people rushed past their squad car, one man nearly running straight into Vance's bumper directly behind them.

In the absence of tourists and park-goers, the circular drive in front of the mansion proper was deathly quiet. The main house of white trimmed in red brick with its matching outbuildings crouched in a forlorn huddle against the snow, fancy teacakes lost in an explosion of white icing. The deceptively peaceful scene sent a shiver up Vikash's back. Unless the stampeding crowd had all reached the same sudden painful epiphany about the meaninglessness of existence and had run off screaming in a mass existential panic, something was lurking nearby.

Vikash scanned the grounds as he got out of the car, unwilling to make a move in any direction yet.

"It's quiet. Too quiet," Kyle muttered the old movie cliché and Vikash had to stifle a nervous snicker.

"We're at about fifty percent humidity." Jeff Gatling came around the car to Vikash's side. "Vance? Got spark?"

Luckily, Vance was intent on the hunt and not on tormenting Kyle. He held up a hand, fingers pointed skyward. Smoke curled up, then a dark puff erupted before flames danced over his fingertips. "Oh, yeah. We got spark. Bring it on."

"Contain if we can," Jeff admonished softly. "Incinerate as a last resort. You hear me, Vance?"

His partner grumbled, but joined them as they all retrieved nets and bags from their squad cars. Movement caught the edge of Vikash's sight. He turned slowly and spotted a quick flash of something vanishing behind the outbuilding on the left.

"There." He pointed, moving slowly but deliberately across the snow.

"Did you see it, Kash? How big?" Kyle moved out a few feet to the left, in case their culprit decided to flee.

Vikash shook his head. "Didn't see enough."

The snow was new enough not to have a crunch to it yet, muffling their steps as they worked their way around the building, Vikash and Kyle to the left, Jeff and Vance to the right. When the thing broke cover, it did so with alarming speed, barreling from behind the building and knocking Kyle to the ground before rolling over him.

"Kyle?" Vikash called, even as he tried to herd the thing back to Jeff and Vance.

"'M all right."

While Vikash wasn't convinced, he couldn't go back to check on his partner yet. Seven feet in diameter, the bizarre apparition that had caused a stampede appeared to be a giant ball of horticultural debris. It rolled and bounced toward the river, sticks, dried leaves and vines all tangled and prickling unevenly along its surface like a bad haircut. With his longer legs, Vikash outdistanced his colleagues easily and so was directly in the line of fire when the tumbleweed of madness stopped abruptly, shook itself, and hurled a mass of stick missiles his way. He dove to the side, his jacket taking the brunt of the assault. Behind him, he heard a sharp cry of pain.

The tumbleweed rustled again, apparently readying a second volley. Vikash covered his head and risked a glance back at Jeff, sprawled on the ground with a two-inch diameter stick embedded in his shoulder.

Vance rose from where he had knelt beside his partner, his face scarlet as he bellowed, "Fucking freakazoid!"

Flames shot from his fingers when he flung out one arm then the other, ten-foot gouts of flame that threatened to set the trees on fire as Vance raced toward the tumbleweed. With smoke rising from several fire strikes, the creature fled in erratic bounces across Kelly Drive until it reached the Playing Angels sculpture beside the river. For a moment, Vikash was afraid it would leap into the river, but it cowered behind the three horn-playing angels on their tall plinths, dodging from one to another as Vance kept up his barrage.

"Vance!" Jeff called, struggling to sit up. "Knock it off! Containment!"

But Vance ignored him, muttering a stream of invectives about freaks firing on law enforcement. While sometimes it could be a tough call dealing with nonhuman lawbreakers, their standing orders were to detain unless the creature posed an imminent threat. To Vikash at least, it was clear that the tumbleweed was more frightened than malicious. He slammed into Vance, tackling him into the snow beneath the right-hand angel while Kyle tried to beat out the spreading flames with his jacket.

Even with blood spreading down his blue uniform shirt, Jeff joined the fire suppression effort, though it seemed hopeless. The flames popped and snapped, and a terrible, frightened wailing came from the center of the tumbleweed.

"Get off me, you jackass!" Vance bucked and squirmed, but he was clearly still out of control, so Vikash wasn't going to let him up yet. He had to duck a fist aimed at his head and was just about to use his longer limbs to pin Vance's arms in a bear hug when their fire starter suddenly went limp.

His eyes flew open, pupils blown, staring at something behind Vikash. His fear was so real that Vikash shot a glance over his shoulder, but saw only the blindingly clear blue of a winter sky. Carefully, he lifted his weight off. "Vance? What is it?"

"Oh my fucking God. It can't be," Vance whispered as he stood and bent to pick up a nonexistent object from the ground. He took a defensive stance, unresponsive to Vikash's shaking and shouting in his ear. "No! Fucking flying lizards! You can't be here!"

Vance swung wildly with whatever imaginary weapon he held, trying to knock something equally imaginary out of the air. Uncertain whether he should knock Vance back down or simply let him work through his hallucination, Vikash backed up against the statue's concrete plinth.

"Kash! What the hell is going on over there? We could use—"

Between one word and the next, Kyle's voice cut off. The park vanished and Vikash stood blinking in a place of blinding light and strange sounds.

"Kyle?" he called out in helpless anguish, choking on his fear. Something had happened. He was hallucinating as Vance had been. *Stand still. Just stand still and let Kyle come and collect you. Don't panic. This has to be temporary.*

"Greets. Do you need help?"

Vikash startled and spun toward the voice. A vision in a loose flowing robe stood beside him, smiling, green eyes gazing at him with guileless compassion. Long red hair tumbled over the vision's shoulders and though Vikash found himself unable to parse gender, the person's face was achingly familiar. "Kyle?"

"No. I'm Cirrus. But I could be Kyle if you wanted me to be." Cirrus laughed, and even the low, sensual sound was like Kyle's when he was flirting. "Are you a reenactor? Did you get separated from your vid crew?"

"Ah. Hmm." Vikash took in his surroundings now that his eyes had adjusted, feeling stupider by the moment. They stood on a gleaming white porcelain-like surface that moved smoothly under their feet. Huge spires of glass and chrome soared overhead, occupying most of the sky. What little sky he could see was an unrelenting blue, even more painfully bright than the winter sky he had just left behind in the park.

"You're really lost, aren't you?"

"Lost. Yes," Vikash murmured as they passed a window display of colored, porous blocks.

"Oh, you're hungry! That explains the glassy-eyed look." Cirrus's laugh was brighter this time, happy and uninhibited. He...she...grabbed Vikash's hand and hurried down the moving sidewalk. "You don't want to eat there. The prots are way too chalky. I know a place where the food is to *die* for."

Unable to come up with a good argument, Vikash allowed the towing. Other pedestrians stared, but they seemed more intrigued than hostile and their attention focused on his uniform rather than the joined hands. "I… Where?"

"Where are we going? Just around the corner. It's not far."

"No, where…" *I don't want to ask this question. I really don't.* "Where am I?"

Cirrus stopped and considered him a moment. "You mean what street?"

"Am I still on Earth?"

The next laugh cut off on a shocked exclamation. "You're *serious*, aren't you?" Cirrus turned his hand over, stroking the skin of his wrist carefully. "Did you take something new today? You really shouldn't take drugs from strangers."

"No…" Vikash took in the people rushing past, some in simple robes like his guide, many in no more than what amounted to shiny Brazilian thongs. "I think I've been…displaced somehow. Philadelphia. That's where I was last."

"This is Philadelphia." Cirrus's eyes narrowed. "I bet I know what this is. You're doing a historical piece. Twentieth, twenty-first century maybe? And they have some new skin tabs that'll get you all the way in character. But you got away from your crew. Poor thing. No wonder you're all disoriented."

"Historical."

"That's right."

"What century is this?"

"Twenty-third, silly. No, I'm sorry." Cirrus took his hand again and resumed their hurried pace. "That's not fair. You don't know that right now. Don't worry. I'll stay with you and if it doesn't wear off in a couple of hours, we'll get you to a care center. Look, you don't have an emergency contact on your implants somewhere?"

"Implants?"

"They were thorough, I'll give them that. I'm going to have a few words for your crew when we find them." Cirrus flashed him another unnervingly Kyle-esque smile before tugging him toward what appeared to be a solid pane of glass.

Vikash balked, pulling back until Cirrus' leading hand and shoulder passed through the barrier. "How…" But *how did you know that was a door* seemed too ridiculous a question to ask, so he shut up in favor of observing. If he truly had slipped through time somehow, he needed to learn quickly, to cling to small familiarities, or go mad.

The room Cirrus pulled him into was brightly lit, with colorful abstract mosaics covering walls curved into nooks, grottoes and miniature indoor caverns. People gathered around fluted pedestals topped by what appeared to be garish flowers with long, phallic pistils. Most of the occupants, regardless of age, wore little to nothing. No one hid rolls or sagging due to aging, everyone completely comfortable regardless of body type. Vikash found himself acutely embarrassed and uncertain about where it was polite to focus. He ended up staring at his shoes.

Cirrus towed him to an unoccupied pedestal flower. "The savory prot is the best here, but the spicy ones are good, too. Or would you rather a veg?"

"Um?"

"Pretty sure you're having a nutritional crash." Cirrus patted his hand and considered the odd, cinnamon-and-chartreuse flower in front of them. "One of each, I think. What's your name, handsome?"

"Vikash."

"Pretty name. How unusual."

Fingers held under the end of one of the pistils, which all looked identical to Vikash, Cirrus kept still while the opening extruded a pasty orange substance in a perfect cube. The process was repeated with six different pistils — red, green, blue, purple, neon yellow and rainbow-striped cubes joining the orange. Cirrus placed each cube on a round ceramic tray then offered the whole selection to Vikash. He took the tray, trying not to gape, though a careful glance around showed other people eating the things. Apparently, this was twenty-third-century food.

He picked up the orange — perhaps the closest to an actual food color — and bit off a corner. The texture was odd, a cross between a mousse and a macaron, but there were hints of almond and sesame, cardamom and ginger. The rest went down in two eager bites.

"Good, huh? Better than that stuff you'd get at Serra's." Cirrus pulled the robe off, revealing a candy apple red thong beneath. Flat chested, slender, Vikash still wasn't certain.

"I'm sorry. I don't mean to be rude, but what pronoun do you use?"

"Pronoun?" Cirrus obtained a blue cube and popped it in whole.

"He? She? Them?"

"Oh, now you're just shining the polys for fun."

Vikash nibbled at the blue cube, picking up hints of fruit though he couldn't tell what kind. "I have no idea what that means."

Cirrus shook his head, his beautiful thick mane of hair a counterpoint to his disbelief. "They can't have... Did they really block out everything? I mean, that's taking realism in production just a little too far."

"I don't know what's happened to me. Please. I think...I don't know anything."

"Hope those drugs don't have any lasting aftereffects. Poor thing." Cirrus turned a wrist over and pressed just under the palm. "There."

A holographic image appeared, yellow characters hovering over pale skin. Vikash made out the name on top, Cirrus Fairmount-Forty. The next line might have been an address, he couldn't be certain, then another name, Agate Fishtown-Thirtynine. The last line was a completely unhelpful number designation, A-15-1. His face must have shown his confusion, since Cirrus explained the information carefully, full name, dwelling, emergency contact.

"And my gendersex designation," Cirrus smiled, pointing to the A-15-1. "Nothing? Doesn't mean anything to you?"

"No. I'm sorry."

Cirrus waved a hand. "It's just interesting, the things a person takes for granted. The A is my chromosomal-bio designation. So I'm XY and only have male reproductive parts. B would be XX with female parts. C is XXY with only female parts and so on. The fifteen is my neuro-gender number. Fifteen out of thirty-two. My brain scans show both male and female traits, but slightly more male. So I prefer *he,* but for formal situations it's *vre,* of course."

"Of...course." Vikash's head spun with the sheer number of genders the future had. "The one? At the end?"

"Oh, that's the sexuality designation. I'm pan, so it's a one. But I do have a type." Cirrus's lowered gaze and coy little smile could only have been flirting. "Long, lean and confused."

Vikash managed a strangled chuckle, though the humor didn't calm him as it would have with Kyle. *I wish he were here. If I was going to hallucinate like this, why couldn't my brain have brought the actual Kyle instead of a look-alike? I hope it ends soon so I can go home.* But what if it wasn't a hallucination? What if Vance had been experiencing hallucinations prior to an actual time transport? What if he was in the Jurassic? *Physically* there now? Then maybe Vikash had been transported as well, through some strange paranormal mechanism, doorway, wormhole, gateway. What if he could never get home?

"You went all glassy again," Cirrus was saying softly, rubbing his back. "It's going to be all right. I can take you to a care center if you're not feeling well. Or would you rather go fuck? There's a sex salon two doors down. It might help you relax. I'm certified in both therapeutic and emergency sex."

"No. Thank you. For offering." Retreating behind a polite mask made answering easier, but the shock of such a casual offer, loudly, in public, made him feel like a stammering teenager. Maybe if he could lie down somewhere and go to sleep, he might wake up back home. Or maybe he had to die in the hallucination. Hadn't he read that in a story once? *What am I going to do?*

He must have whispered it aloud, since Cirrus flung his arms around Vikash to hug him tight. "Poor lost data set. Finish your lunch and I'll take you over to Central Care. I'm putting out an alert to see which production company misplaced you. They really should have their historical license suspended."

Vikash could only nod and do as he was told. If some accident had truly displaced him, he was a nonperson here, with no voice and a child's knowledge of the world. How would he live? Would he want to? Two centuries in the future meant everyone he knew was long dead—his family, his cat, Kyle.

He had to swallow against the hard lump in his throat. What good was seeing the wonders of the future if he had to do it without Kyle?

Chapter Two

Back on the strange porcelain sidewalk, which Cirrus explained was really an impact-resistant polyceramic, Vikash did his best to pay attention. The sheer variety of personal transport, from floating scooters to self-driven cars, and the overload of strange buildings proved too much, though. His brain kept trying to drift off into daydreams of home, of familiar things, unable to process so much new all at once.

Faint, ethereal notes tugged him back to his future present and it took several moments to register that the music was coming from Cirrus.

"'Scuse a sec," Vikash's little guide murmured as he lifted his arm and tapped on his wrist. An image of a person in miniature appeared above his arm, a person with a decidedly...blue complexion. Cirrus' smile warmed, the person obviously known and the contact welcome. "Greets, XK410. Howzit?"

"Greetings, Cirrus. All is well." The person's voice was deep and resonant, at odds with the tiny projection. "Though I am reassessing the new features."

"I thought you might soon. Face time to go over options? I gave you schedule access, right?"

"Thank you. I hope you're not offended."

"No, no! This is about you being happy with the modifications. I'll see you soon." Cirrus tapped again to end the call and turned his sunny smile on Vikash. "Client. Sorry. I'm an AI consultant."

Right. His guide wouldn't spend his days just picking up strays and offering sex. "You program AIs?"

Cirrus' smile vanished in a wide-eyed expression of shock. "That's...obscene. Of course not. I would never disrespect an AI like that."

"Ah." The agreement was automatic. Vikash had no idea how programming would be offensive. "What do you do?"

Still regarding him sideways, Cirrus said, "I'm an aesthetic consultant, of course. I help AIs with anthro issues. It's tough for them to judge things on a human aesthetic scale, so I help."

Anthro? Anthropomorphic? Oh. Finally things rattled into place. The client with the blue skin was an AI, one with a humanoid appearance. So Cirrus was a robotic fashion consultant? "Clothes?"

"Sure. Though only when asked. My clients mostly need help with facial features and hands. Hands are tricky."

Automatically, Vikash looked at his hands, the long, bronze fingers. Then he thought of Kyle's—square, strong and scarred. Hands did offer unexpected clues and cues. "I can see that."

Cirrus nodded, lips pursed as he scanned some sort of list on his implanted wrist device. "I think 410's probably not happy with the nose we decided on. Maybe something more classical." His head jerked around. "Like yours. Could I take a schematics scan?

Would you mind entering that beautiful, regal nose in the catalogs?"

"Um." All the so-far-out-of-left-field-he-needed-a-bigger-glove questions were making his head ache. "Will it hurt?"

"Storm holes! Of course not." Cirrus snagged his sleeve and guided him onto an intersecting walkway that shuttled them down a cross street. "Just a scan. But if you don't want your nose replicated, I understand. It truly is beautiful."

Vikash reached for his nose self-consciously. He felt a bit as if he were undergoing dissection. Serviceable, his nose, but he had always thought it was too long. One of his sisters said he looked like a greyhound. "It's fine. You can. Thank you."

At a building of opaque black glass, Cirrus tugged at him again and Vikash stumbled as they left the moving walkway, cringing as he slammed his elbow into the doorway. It nearly brought tears to his eyes, not because of the pain but because it verified for him how real his situation was. Hallucinations didn't come with such sharp sensations.

"Careful. All right?"

Vikash could only nod, trying to find a calm space in spinning thoughts that were clearly circling the drain. "I'm… Is this a hospital?"

"Much nicer than those old meat factories. No one's going to do horrid things to you here like cut you open or inject you full of radioactive isotopes."

I think he just called twenty-first century medicine primitive. And I'm not certain I can even be offended. Cirrus led him through a brightly lit tunnel corridor, its walls decorated in bright primary color chaos, and down to a seating area with plump, comfortable settees and couches. Rather than them waiting to be acknowledged by an overworked intake staffer behind a forbidding desk, a pleasant young woman approached with a thin, transparent film in her right hand.

"Are you in crisis?" Her voice was soft and cheerful, calming rather than sharply authoritative.

Cirrus patted his arm. "This is Vikash. He is."

"Physical, emotional or spiritual?" she asked, pressing a corner of her sheet until it glowed. Compassion and patience warmed her gaze as she waited expectantly, her fingers hovering over the sheet.

"I don't..." Vikash wanted to tell her that crisis seemed extreme, but the words became trapped in the silver discs of her eyes. *AI.*

She nodded and tapped at the glowing film. "All three. Please proceed down the green pathway to Room Twelve."

He knew better than to expect something cold and clinical from this friendly, comfort-driven world, but he still stopped in the doorway, gaping. Instead of institutional green or blue, the walls were the deep, rich green of pine needles, covered in some pliant textile rather than painted. Vikash's fingers sank into the surface when he touched it. The mocha-colored floor gave as well when he stepped on it, though the material used was more springy than spongy.

Along one wall, a piece of furniture lounged in regal splendor. Vikash supposed one might call it a reclining couch, though it was broad enough for three people. Covered in a green several shades darker than the walls, it had several attached dispensers similar to the ones in the strange restaurant or food court or whatever the place of nourishing cubes was called.

"Lie down and rest, Vikash." Cirrus pulled him toward the couch-bed. "You're obviously in lactic acid overload. I can almost hear your muscles screaming."

"Shoes? Do I strip?"

Cirrus blinked at him as if he'd asked if he could take off his head. "Whatever makes you comfortable. I can see why you might want to take those shoes off. They look like torture."

I like the chukkas. Most comfortable shoes I ever owned. Vikash sat on a ledge beside the couch-bed and pulled off his ankle boots. Rude to put street shoes up on the furniture. When he sat on the bed, he twitched as the surface sank under him, molding around to cradle his butt. The couch hug was disconcerting and yet oddly comfortable.

"It won't...try to hold me?" Vikash poked at the couch, watching his finger sink into the green.

"Of course it holds you. It's supposed to soothe you and diag—oh!" Cirrus' hands fluttered, little birds of negation. "I see. No. It won't try to keep you still. If you need to get up, it'll help you."

Vikash nodded and lay back. Part of him wanted to run screaming, his culture-shocked brain overloading, but that would have been rude. Polite. Calm. That's what the outside world needed to see, no matter what world. He sank into the couch, the cushion reacting to his contours and embracing him, cradling and supporting him in all the right places. When he shivered, the material around him warmed as a low-frequency vibration began around his lower back and shoulders.

"It...does feel nice."

"Of course it does." Cirrus stroked his hair as if touching a stranger so intimately was perfectly normal. "Just relax and let the unit do its work. Don't you have someone we can call? Could you pull up your ident listings for me?"

"I don't...have that."

"Don't be silly. Everyone has idents." Gently, Cirrus took his arm and turned it over to examine his wrist. He stroked and prodded, his pale skin fading to parchment. "Howling storm holes. You don't. You... How can that even be possible?"

"I'm not from around here?"

Cirrus's hands flew in bird mode again before settling on either side of his face. "All right. It's all right. No wonder you've looked shocky this whole time. The unit's going to help you rest. Just go to sleep. I'm calling central assistance. They'll have someone down here to help find out where you belong before you wake up. You poor thing. That production company's not going to have its license by tomorrow. I'll make sure."

I don't want to be placed. They won't find me in any database. What's going to happen to me? "I think..." But any protest Vikash might have made drifted off in a gray marshmallow haze. The damn couch unit had drugged him. *One hundred...ninety-nine...ninety-eight...*

* * * *

Bright light turned the inside of Vikash's eyelids scarlet. He didn't want to open his eyes. They had moved him somewhere new and even the recent familiarity of Cirrus would be gone. *Just a little longer. I'll just pretend to be asleep so I don't have to answer questions yet or be told again how lost and primitive I am.*

A rustling came from his left. The sound of pages turning? Then a voice began to read, "Mirrim roused Menolly early the next—"

"Kyle?" Vikash surged up, dizzy and blinking against the sunlight. He couldn't see. The room pitched and his rusty voice cracked as he called out desperately, "Kyle!"

"Hey, hey, I'm here." A strong hand closed over his shoulder, urging him to lie back. "I'm here, Kash. You're all right. Easy. Easy now."

His head rose as someone adjusted the bed and he rubbed at his eyes, trying to focus through force of will, his heart thudding out a fevered step dance. The light wasn't some strange examination light but sunlight streaming through the window of a bland room of white and chrome.

"Hospital?" he croaked out.

"Yeah, you got it. Deep breath." Kyle's voice retreated, but only as far as a blurred chair by the bed.

"Not a care center?"

"Not a...what? Kash, settle down. You're okay. You're in a hospital room at St. Joseph's. They admitted you when you wouldn't wake up."

"Kyle..." Finally, Vikash could see him, see the bright sun-sparks in Kyle's hair, his restless, acid-burned hands clutching the book he had been reading. "I don't... Was I gone?"

Kyle's eyebrows drew together and he let out an explosive breath. "Gone? You were out cold. Unresponsive."

"Physically? Did I vanish?" Frantic, Vikash groped for a hand, his heart finally slowing when Kyle's fingers closed over his. That hand. He knew that hand. It was really Kyle's.

"Um. Vanish? No." Kyle's stroked his thumb over Vikash's knuckles, his rough skin better than the softest caress. "Where do you think you would've gone?"

His throat was too tight to answer yet. He settled for squeezing Kyle's hand tighter. Footsteps in the hall made him jerk away, and though he tried to cover the automatic social twitch by adjusting his position in bed, Kyle wasn't fooled. Hurt radiated from him, the way his smile vanished and he pulled away, slouched down in his chair.

"*Dragonsong*?" Vikash asked in a desperate attempt to sidestep the argument they had both been avoiding.

Kyle glanced down at the book, the older cover with the stylized waves Vikash recognized as his own copy. "Heh. Yeah. I figured if I talked to you, you might find your way back. But I ran out of things to say."

A little smile tugged at Vikash's lips despite his distress. "You? Never."

"Funny guy. It was just easier to read something so I didn't look like a nutcase talking to myself. And I figured I might as well pick something we both like." Kyle leaned forward with the book in both hands. "You're safe, Kash. Promise."

An odd squeak came from behind Kyle and he lifted his jacket from the back of the chair as a fuzzy…something poked out of the inside pocket. Kyle put his hand out and the black-striped purple fuzz crawled onto his palm, wrapping one end of its caterpillar-like form around his wrist.

Maybe I didn't wake up after all. Maybe this is just another hallucination. Maybe I'm not home at all. "Kyle?" He hated how his voice wavered and broke, but he was at the end of his emotional rope.

"Sorry. This little guy was at the center of the tumbleweed monster. We're not sure what he is, but he's been a big help."

"Um."

"Kash, this is Tim."

Vikash pulled back, wary of the creature held out to him. "Tim?"

"Jeff named him. After Tim the Enchanter from Monty Python? Since he seemed so big and bad and wasn't." Kyle chuckled at his blank expression. "It's a

Jeff thing, I guess. After we rescued him from the fire, Tim was very polite. He pointed out that both you and Vance had these, um, bugs, attached to you. Yours was behind your ear. Vance's was right under his shirt collar."

"Bugs." Vikash twisted the institutional white blanket between his hands, suddenly too aware of wearing nothing but a saggy, blue-polka-dotted hospital gown. "Linear, maybe? Please?"

"Sorry, sorry." Kyle held up both hands and Tim squeaked in protest, clinging tighter to his wrist. "Overexcited 'cause you woke up. You know how I get."

"Yes." Vikash settled more comfortably against the bed, trying to accept that he was home, in the correct timeline. "We went to Fairmount Park to answer a disturbance call. Chased the tumbleweed. Jeff got a stick lodged in his shoulder."

Tim let out a sorrowful chirp and Kyle petted his fuzz with one finger. "It's okay. Jeff wasn't badly hurt. You were scared."

Odd development. Vikash wondered if Tim was living with Kyle now, or just along to visit. He cleared his throat and continued, trying to encourage his more verbal partner into more of a report mode. "We approached, ah, Tim inside his now-burning tumbleweed at the Playing Angels. Vance suddenly began to shout about flying lizards and attempting to strike nonexistent things from the air with a nonexistent object. At this point I...went somewhere else."

Kyle nodded. "You did. Vance was yelling and being a hazard to everyone around him, but you just stood there and, yeah, went away. You wandered a little bit, but you weren't seeing anything, not even a hand waved in front of your face, or hearing me yelling for you. It just…you looked scared. As much as you can look scared, Mr. Statue Face. But then Vance keeled over, twitching. Few seconds later, you did, too. Scared the hell out of me. Jeff's trying to pull Tim out of the burning wreckage of his tumbleweed, so now he's bleeding *and* burned, so I've got three officers down. I'm yelling into the radio for ambulance and backup. It was a total clusterfuck."

"I'm sorry."

"Shh." Kyle waved with the Tim-free hand. "Nothing you could have done. My poor Kash, twitching in the snow." He heaved a shaking breath, but kept his smile from slipping. "Yeah, you worried me. But you're back. Wanna tell me what happened?"

"No." Vikash shivered, unable to shake his disorientation. He glanced over at Kyle's snort. "Not right…now. I was somewhere else. It was…it felt real."

Kyle patted his arm. "I'm sorry. Whatever this was really freaked you out. We'll get you and Vance together —"

Tim emitted a strange rumble, almost a growl.

"Oh, he is not *that* bad." Kyle turned to scold his strange passenger. "I'm sure he's not going to set you on fire ever again." Shaking his head, he addressed Vikash again. "Anyway. Get you two to compare notes. We think whatever happened was because of the bugs Tim found on you. But Vance hasn't woken up yet and we're just guessing right now."

"Kyle." Vikash waited until Kyle had stilled, looking at him expectantly. "I was scared I couldn't make it back to you."

"Seriously, Kash?" Kyle ran a hand back over his head, unconsciously spiking his hair in a way that made Vikash's heart constrict. "You're gonna say things like that to me here? Where you won't let me even hold hands?"

"I'm so—"

"You're sorry. I know." Kyle stood, easing Tim back into his jacket pocket. "I *know*. But I wanna climb up into that bed and hold you, you understand? Kiss you until that lost look in your eyes goes away. It's killing me not to."

Vikash could only nod. He was doing it again, shutting down, backing off instead of trying to fix things, as he had with every previous relationship. His last girlfriend had called him Iceman. The boyfriend before that had accused him of being an android. But anyone could walk in on them. He couldn't fix this now.

"Fine. I can't really pick on a guy in a hospital bed." Kyle's smile was there, but it looked painted on. "That wouldn't be fair. Gonna tell the nurses you're awake. I have to run Tim back to the station. He just wanted to see how you were doing, I think. And then I'll swing by your place to check on Ellie. If they do something crazy like discharge you this evening, you'll call me, right?"

"Of course." He wanted to say more, so much more, but Kyle was already walking out of the door with a little wave.

Damn it. Kyle was the best thing to have happened to him since…maybe ever. He was screwing this all up and he wasn't sure he could stop. The things Kyle wanted—to be open and out as a couple—Vikash couldn't give him. Not while they were police partners. But would it have killed him to let Kyle, who had obviously been worried sick, hold his hand? Maybe kiss him goodbye? Too much control in public, he was too accustomed to it, hiding his reactions, hiding his thoughts.

It's not as if Kyle's begging to climb you like an apple tree in public. But mixing professional and private life even as little as they had been was precarious at best, with disaster the inevitable conclusion. Vikash sighed, too tired to see a way through.

A nurse bustled in to take vitals and ask questions, followed a few minutes later by an intern who did some basic neurological tests and told Vikash his EEG from that morning looked good and his CAT scan was clear. He felt shaky and lightheaded when they got him up to walk a few steps, but otherwise he didn't seem to have lingering symptoms.

With the initial round of medical bustle complete and a bland, unappetizing dinner set on the tray in front of him, Vikash found himself shivering in reaction. He hadn't even asked how long he'd been out or thanked Kyle for sitting with him and for taking care of his cat. Scattered. Unfocused. He kept waiting for some unknown piece of technology to appear and confirm that he hadn't really made it back.

"Officer Soren."

Startled, he jerked his head around to see Lieutenant Dunfee standing in the doorway. "Ma'am?"

"I hear you're refusing to report on your experience."

Vikash sat up straighter, pulling his blanket up as far as possible. "Refusing?"

"We had a PPI out there in the park, Soren. I expect full cooperation and communication from my officers." She stalked across the floor and perched on the chair by the bed.

Possible Paranormal Incident and he had refused to tell Kyle... *Oh.* "I would have, ma'am," he offered and it sounded like an excuse even in his own ears.

"Hmm." She stood again, paced to the locker-closet on the wall and began tossing his clothes to him.

"Monroe seemed to think you weren't comfortable here, so I've convinced them to discharge you." With a solid *thunk*, she dropped his boots next to the bed then reached up to draw the curtain. From the other side, she ordered, "Verbal report, Soren, while you get dressed. I'll drive you home."

"Um…" Vikash slid out of bed, fumbling for his underwear.

"Any day now. I don't have all night."

He cleared his throat and tried to turn on his professional side, even as he stood naked except for his briefs, trying to get his pants legs turned the right way around. Bit by bit, in short sentences, he related his dislocation adventure, though he left out the offer of emergency sex. Some things the lieutenant didn't need to know. He shoved the curtain aside when he was pulling on his shoes, and found himself confronted with her darkest frown.

"Ma'am?"

"At least you seem functional. Virago's having a post-trauma reaction. He's convinced a pteranadon chomped off his right arm. The doctors tell me the pain is very real for him."

"Is it gone?" Vikash asked in horror. "His arm?"

"No. It's still there. He's physically unharmed." Her frown deepened as she held out his jacket to him. "Your bodies stayed here. And while he was in the Cretaceous and you were somewhere in the future, both of you seem to have been through something too vivid to be hallucinations. A mental displacement."

"It was these, ah, bugs?"

She nodded. "They secrete venom, for lack of a better word. Our lab folks found the poison in your bloodstream and in Virago's."

"Any idea of origin? Any other cases reported?"

An almost-smile twitched at her lips. "Attaboy. Now you're thinking again. Tonight, we get you home to rest. Tomorrow, you can start finding answers for me."

Chapter Three

Light puddled out from under the door when Vikash climbed the steps to his second-floor apartment. The knob turned under his hand when he tried it. "Kyle?"

"Hey! Look who's home, Ellie. I'm in the kitchen!"

Something smelled wonderful and familiar, but his tired brain couldn't quite place it. A white puffball careened around the corner, arrowing toward him with frantic squeaks. Vikash scooped her up, rubbing his face against her thick white ruff and immediately getting fur in his mouth. Anxiety shed. Poor Ellie.

A purring Ellie tucked up in the crook of his right arm, trying to clear fur from his tongue with his left hand, Vikash meandered through the living room to the kitchen where Kyle was clanking around. Bowl-shaped takeout containers sat empty on the counter, the contents presumably in the pots on the stove. The delicious scent finally found a name in Vikash's tired brain.

"You got us Han Dynasty?"

"Yeah. Lieutenant said she'd bring you home and I figured you needed some comfort food. Dan-dan noodles in the yellow pot, the cumin chicken you love in the silver. The garlic sauce tofu for me."

"Cold chili noodles?"

Kyle finally turned from the stove, his voice cracking. "In the fridge. Kash, put the damn cat down."

The cat? Oh. Carefully, he placed Ellie on the floor, then held his arms wide. He expected Kyle to throw himself into them, but he just stood there, looking stricken. Right. Passive invitation wasn't much of an apology, after all. He closed the distance between them to wrap his arms hard around a stiff, resisting Kyle.

"Damn it, Kash." The resistance only lasted a moment. Kyle's head came to rest on his shoulder, one arm wrapped around Vikash's waist. "Just…damn it."

"I'm sorry," Vikash whispered into Kyle's hair. Not able to voice a coherent apology, he let his arms speak for him as he held his partner tightly.

Kyle grunted, whether in acknowledgment or because his ribs were creaking. Without raising his head, he muttered, "Don't need your apologies, Soren. You're gonna eat your damn dinner and you're gonna tell me what the hell happened."

"Did you tell the lieutenant I refused?"

"She asked me if you'd told me and I said no. Don't turn this into me tattling."

"I… Sorry."

"What the hell did I just say?"

"Yes. Um." Vikash disentangled, disturbed that Kyle still sounded so irritated. Usually, holding Kyle had the opposite effect. "I'll, ah, get bowls."

Despite his shaking hands and Kyle's exasperated sounds, Vikash dished up rice for both of them, filled his bowl with the cumin and Kyle's with the tofu, and brought both noodle dishes to the table. Kyle grumbled, but settled for bringing them both beer, and they seated themselves at the table in the dining room in silence.

Ellie hopped up on her designated chair, expecting to share, but when Vikash let her sniff at the spicy food, she sneezed and fled. Gradually, his shaking subsided. Softly, in halting sentences, he told Kyle about the future, the one he had visited at any rate. From his first moment of panic to his anguished thoughts that he would never get home as he'd drifted off to sleep. For Kyle, he tried to tell all of it, not just the facts. Everything that was said, everything he saw or touched or tasted, even what he had been thinking.

"Little guy looked like me, huh?" Kyle finally spoke, head still over his food.

"He did. But it wasn't."

"You're really not doing well with this, are you?"

"No."

"What's going on in that hedge maze of a brain, Kash? You're back with us. You're fine."

Vikash put his bowl down. The chili noodles had heated his lips to the point of pain and it felt so good. Real. "What if...what if I go to sleep tonight and...dislocate again? What if I can't get back?"

"You're afraid of going to sleep."

"Afraid of slipping away. Of everything slipping away. I was in the future."

Kyle moved his chair closer to put his hand on Vikash's arm. "I almost hate to say it, but it sounded kinda cool."

"It wasn't cool!" The volume of his own voice shocked Vikash. He froze, mouth working, fighting to breathe before he could whisper, "Everyone was dead. You were dead."

"Shit." Kyle's eyes widened as he swallowed hard. His hand still clutching Vikash's arm, he slid to his knees to put his head in Vikash's lap. "You poor bastard. Your family. Everyone you know. You thought you'd lost your family and I haven't been taking this seriously."

His hands were shaking again. This never happened to him, this prolonged imbalance. He took Kyle's face between his palms, lifting his head so he could look into those bright green eyes. "*You* were dead. Do you hear me?"

"I hear you," Kyle whispered, his eyes glistening with things unsaid. He tugged Vikash's shirt from his uniform pants—his stay at the hospital hadn't been long enough for someone to bring him a change of clothes—and slid his hands underneath, furnace-hot against Vikash's chilled skin.

Vikash hooked his hands under Kyle's armpits and hauled him up, crashing their lips together in a clumsy, desperate kiss of clicking teeth and overeager tongues. *I need this. I need you, more than I can say.* This, of course, was true, since he couldn't bring himself to say it. He let his hands speak for him, fumbling Kyle's shirt buttons open in hasty, staccato forays, running his hands over the bit of red fur scattered across the center of Kyle's chest. Completely natural, Kyle had never shaved or waxed in his life, so he said, and all his body hair had that ginger tinge Vikash adored.

He had to break the kiss when Kyle gave up on buttons and yanked Vikash's uniform shirt over his head. Scrambling up, Kyle straddled his thighs, bare chests pressed together as he resumed the kiss, plunging his tongue into Vikash's mouth, grinding against him like a horny teenager.

"You're so cold. Damn it, why didn't you say something? We need to get you in bed," Kyle breathed against his ear.

"I'm fine. You're warm." Vikash used the momentary stillness to undo the button fly on Kyle's jeans. He fished Kyle's cock out, stroking the head with his thumb, heat rushing through him at Kyle's gasp. "Stay here."

"Okay." Kyle's voice rasped, hoarse with need. He leaned in to kiss the bridge of Vikash's nose. "But can I take off my pants?"

Vikash let him go but only to allow Kyle to slide from his lap. He hooked his thumbs in the belt loops of Kyle's jeans and eased the denim down to his knees. So often, they were tired and happy to get each other off simply, quickly—a screw in the shower, a sixty-nine before bed. When they did have the time, on those rare weekends not on shift and not on call, Vikash insisted on control. Always. Kyle never seemed to mind and while tussling was often a part of foreplay, he eventually would cede in absolute, eager capitulation.

Tonight was different. Vikash's heart ached that he couldn't let go more, that he wasn't able to match Kyle's *fuck the world, this is who I am* approach to life. It hurt Kyle, it would be the end of them together, and he hated it. He took Kyle by the hips, fingers kneading at the firm mounds of his ass. "Ride me? Here?"

"Get your pants off and let me suck you," Kyle said with a soft smile, the one that made Vikash's bones melt into heated caramel. "No way I'm leaving you to grab lube and you're sure as hell not taking me dry."

That was an impossible-to-resist invitation. Vikash unzipped and shoved his pants and briefs down to the floor, stomping and tugging awkwardly to yank one leg free so Kyle could kneel between his feet.

Kyle gazed up at him for the second time that evening, though now his eyes shone with mischief. With his hands on Vikash's thighs, he pushed them farther apart, leaning in to nuzzle at the black hair beside his balls. "Most gorgeous view in the universe, right here."

"God...Kyle." Vikash tried to bury his fingers in Kyle's hair, but he'd just gotten it cut again and there wasn't a lot to grab.

"Well, if you really want to build an altar to me, I guess I won't complain too much." Kyle hummed as he licked a wet trail up the underside of Vikash's cock, making it twitch. "You smell like hospital. We need to fix that."

"How would—" Vikash cut off in a long moan as Kyle's lips closed over the head of his cock. He fought to keep still, fought to let go. This was Kyle's show and he had to stop trying to control every moment.

Kyle's wicked tongue lapped and stroked as he sucked hard, messy, slurping, wet heat wrapped around Vikash in a way that stopped his brain. He wanted to say something. *Stop, please, more, I won't last,* but all he managed was a ragged moan. Tugging at Kyle's hair did no good. His stubborn partner grinned around Vikash's cock, obviously pleased with himself to have made him come unglued.

Vikash's fingers tightened until the chair arm creaked and Kyle finally took pity on him, sliding up his body and straddling his thighs again.

"Careful," Vikash murmured.

Kyle raised an eyebrow. "Please tell me you're not saying to be gentle with you?"

"I don't want to hurt you."

"Hey." Kyle stroked a hand through his hair. "Stay still. Just enjoy. And I guarantee you won't hurt me any more than I want. Got it?"

Vikash swallowed against a dry throat. He could do this. He was fine when Kyle drove the squad car. He could let him drive here. "Yes."

"Relax. Kash, it's okay." The hand stroking his hair slid down to his shoulder and on to trace the lines of his tattoo. "Your fire lizards look about ready to jump off your skin. Relax. Hands on my hips, just so you have something to hang on to. Help me keep my balance."

"Balance. Right." Vikash closed his eyes, breathing slowly through his nose as Kyle reached back to take him in hand, angling his spit-slick cock at Kyle's tight hole.

Kyle hissed as he lowered himself slowly, grunting as the head breached. He held still, thighs trembling, chin on his chest, and Vikash was about to call a halt when Kyle let his head drop back and slid down farther, taking Vikash into his glorious, tight heat.

"Kash… Oh, damn… You feel so good. Don't move. Not yet. Lemme just…" Kyle put his forehead on Vikash's shoulder with a hard moan, easing up and down Vikash's shaft, working the spit in. His erection had flagged, but now he wrapped his fingers around his own cock, stroking slowly while Vikash watched in rapt adoration, each breath a tortured pant.

"Now? Kyle, please."

"Yeah. Now, love. Move. Split me in two."

Vikash cried out as he gripped Kyle's hips tight enough to bruise and thrust up hard. The legs of the dining room chair thumped against the floor with each forceful stroke. Kyle threw his head back, jacking himself faster with each pump, thumping down into Vikash's lap with every drive up. The ecstasy on his face was beautiful, his eyes squeezed shut, his mouth open as his cries escalated.

Just as Vikash's balls drew tight and his thrusts came in desperate syncopation, Kyle let out a loud "Ha!" and shot white ropes across Vikash's belly and chest. It would have been the perfect moment. It was the perfect moment, until an ominous crack echoed directly under Vikash's ass. One last thrust before he came in hard, mind-battering spasms, and the chair collapsed beneath them, forcing Vikash to wrap his arms tightly around Kyle and try to not to jar him too much as they fell with clatters and thuds to the floor.

They lay still, breathing hard, chair slats poking into Vikash's back at odd angles. "Huh. That's the last time I buy one of those self-assembled chairs."

With the softening cock still inside him, Kyle buried his face against Vikash's chest and laughed until he couldn't breathe.

Chapter Four

Larry the ghost whistled softly as he made coffee, carafe and filter floating through the air seemingly unsupported. No one ever drank the terrible coffee Larry made, but the act of making it prevented him from going poltergeist, so the coffee and filters went on the squad's expenses.

In his corner with his perch and his drawing paper tacked to the wall, Edgar worked on a new red ink masterpiece with the pen clutched tight in his left foot claws, his swearing only occasional soft mutters. Krisk the lizard man hissed at his computer, tail swishing against the floor as he worked. Greg and Shira bickered in whispers across the room, something about taking the last chocolate doughnut, while Amanda listened with half an ear to Carrington's complaints about his most recent conquest gone wrong.

It was good to be back in the squad room. Vikash had been gone only two days, but it felt like so much longer, a homecoming warmth sliding through him as he placed his coffee – purchased outside – on its proper coaster on his half of the desk across from Kyle.

Familiar. Right. The world was beginning to steady again and he had work to do.

Vance was still in the hospital, apparently sedated much of the time, and Jeff was still on medical leave while his hands and shoulder healed. Tim, on the other hand, had moved into the station house, happily gathering up shredded paper from the copier wastebasket to make himself a new, softer tumbleweed which he used to roll around from room to room. He had attended morning roll call, cleaned up crumbs in the break room and generally seemed content to stay.

"Our first mascot." Kyle chuckled as he followed Tim's rolling progress across the floor to pick up a dropped Post-it note beside Wolf's chair.

"Larry?"

"No, Tim. Larry came with the building, as I understand it. Or maybe with one of the old squad cars the 77th inherited. Besides, Larry was a cop. Can't call him a mascot."

Vikash nodded. He supposed that wasn't very respectful, though he didn't say so since his attention had already jogged off in another direction. "Did the bugs go to the lab? Or to SPU?"

Kyle's head jerked around. "No. I mean, we still have them here. State Paranormal Unit didn't seem that interested when we sent photos."

"I need to see them."

"Fair enough. They're not much to look at, though. Fair warning."

Kyle got up, but instead of walking back toward the evidence room, he weaved his way through the desks to the workstation Carrington and Amanda shared.

What in the world? Kyle stood back a bit from the desk, probably to avoid absorbing rather dubious powers from their coworkers. It would only be for a few hours, but Kyle said that sharing Carrington's thirst for washed platelet blood was uncomfortable and 'fucking weird'. Their squad's vampire nodded at something Kyle said, and turned to take an object out of the little private minifridge beside his desk. He handed a test tube to Amanda, who rolled her eyes and brought it to Vikash.

"That's the little bastard," Amanda said as she handed it off. "We thought Carr's fridge would be the safest place for them, since no one messes with it. And, you know, it would freak people out to put their lunches next to crazy-hallucination bugs in the break room fridge."

He turned the glass test tube to read the label. *Bug — behind left ear — Soren*. The date, Kyle's initials. But this was his bug, the one that had sent his mind into the future. Possible future. It wasn't at all imposing or strange looking. A segmented brown-gray body about the size of his thumbnail lay curled into a ball at the bottom of the test tube. The little hitchhiker looked exactly like the ones he used to find digging in his mother's garden.

"Pill bug."

"Yeah. That's what I thought, too." Kyle nodded at the test tube. "Pill bugs with drugged time-travel inducing venom."

A flurry of wings announced Edgar's abandonment of his quiet drawing as he landed on the desk beside Vikash and made a grab for the tube.

Vikash held it at arm's length to keep it away. "No, Edgar. You can't put evidence in your hoard. Or suspects. Which this might be, I suppose."

"Goat cheese fucker!" Edgar called out, pacing up and down on the desk and ruffling his feathers.

"Chain of custody doesn't include ravens, I'm sorry." Vikash fished in his top drawer and produced a yellow highlighter. "Here. For your current piece."

Edgar tilted his head back and forth from pill bug test tube to highlighter before he snatched the marker from Vikash's hand with little regard for fingers. "Boneriffic, neckbeard!"

"Really?" Carrington said in an aggrieved tone. "He's polite to Vikash?"

Kyle snickered. "Kinda stretching the definition of polite. But yeah, Kash is polite to everything, so he gets polite back, right?"

"You're his favorite, Carr. So he torments you." Resolving never to leave anything important on top of his desk, Vikash waited until Edgar had resumed his corner perch. "Do we know why my pill bug was…relatively benign and Vance's was so horrific?"

The rest of the officers had gathered around, everyone keeping a respectful distance from Kyle, except Krisk, who hadn't ever activated the Kyle-power vacuuming reaction. At least, never in any noticeable way.

"The lab rats have both the samples." Carrington shrugged as he leaned against the desk, then hissed and yanked his hand out of an early sunbeam. "I doubt they'll find any difference in the venom compositions. But I have a theory."

"Oh, great, here we go," Amanda muttered.

"Hush, Amanda. It's a *good* theory." Carrington pointed a finger toward the ceiling and cringed back from another morning sunbeam piercing the squad room's high, factory-industrial windows. "I think the venom reacts with the victim's psyche. With their emotional matrix, so to speak. Vance is volatile, vitriolic and violent."

"Nice alliteration there, Carr." Greg snickered.

Carrington either didn't register the sarcasm or didn't care. "Thank you. While Vikash? Our Vikash is a sea of calm. Diplomatic and serene. It only makes sense that Vance had a terrible, violent experience while Vikash's was more cerebral."

"So, you're saying the bug venom is like...like LSD or something?" Shira scrunched up her button nose. "State of mind, emotional stuff makes the difference?"

"It seems a reasonable conclusion."

Krisk slammed his tail against the floor, causing Kyle to twitch sideways. With a snarl, Wolf waved at his partner. "I agree with Krisk. It's bullshit. We don't know crap."

He said that with a tail slam? Before tempers could escalate and detonating egos could cause serious damage, Vikash held up a hand. "We are working on limited data. Could I get everyone's help this morning? Please? There might be more cases..."

Amanda nodded even as she fixed Carrington with a quelling look. "We split up the hospitals between us. See what's come through the ER."

A stapler and a tape dispenser fell over on the desk Shira leaned against, but she seemed more excited than nervous, so her broken talent didn't manifest in any larger things flying about. "We can take Tim to check for bugs if we find any cases that sound suspicious."

The shredded paper and Post-it note tumbleweed weaved between police officer legs to the center of their gathering. The purple fuzz that one could only assume was Tim's head popped out as he squeaked enthusiastically.

"I do believe we have Tim's cooperation," Kyle said on a chuckle.

Vikash crouched next to the paper transport system. "Thank you, Tim. We appreciate any help you can give us."

Tim pushed out of the paper farther, and if it were possible for a black-striped purple cylinder of fuzz to come to attention, Vikash had the oddest impression that he did.

Over the next two hours, the squad room hummed with voices in professional mode—phone calls to hospitals and ambulance companies, cross-checks of information, consultations at the whiteboard Vikash had set up to compile findings.

Three suspicious cases had come through the ER. All the potential victims had been outside when they lost consciousness, but none near Mt. Pleasant. One had been close to City Hall, the others near museums. So far, outdoors was the only link they had.

Lieutenant Dunfee, out of her office to see what had her officers working like a beehive, took over assignments as bits of information rolled in. She sent Greg and Shira with Tim to talk to the two victims at St. Joseph's, and Amanda and Carrington to see the one at University Hospital. If the two at St. Joseph's had pill bugs, Tim would find them. Carrington's unnaturally sharp sense of smell would locate the third, if there was one. Wolf and Krisk, never the best choices to talk to witnesses, she sent to Fairmount to sniff around the original incident site.

"Monroe, you and Soren take these newer sites. Witnesses. Surrounding area. What's the connecting link, if there is one." She waved a hand in dismissal. "Let's get out there, folks. Be vigilant, but be thorough. We need to stop this before it gets to the press."

Possible headlines ran through Vikash's thoughts as he tucked his test tube into his shirt pocket and hurried after Kyle to the squad car. *Pill Bug Panic In Philly. Time Travel Trouble Takes Toll.* "Police baffled. Film at eleven."

"What?" Kyle cast an odd look his way, though one corner of his mouth twitched up.

"Thinking out loud. Press."

As usual, Kyle managed to clip on to his leaping thoughts and ride along. "Yeah. Glad I'm not the one going in front of the press horde if they get hold of this. It'll be a nightmare."

It was another one of those surreally beautiful days with a sky too bright a blue and the air sharp enough to slice butter. Philadelphia waffled between two types of weather in February—these bitingly bright ones and the gray depression blankets that heralded wet snow or sleet. Kyle pulled into a spot on Eakins Oval, their first stop, with the art museum looming in the background. The intimidating grand steps were more famous than the museum, simply because of a movie reference, and Vikash had always found that a shame. He tried not to resent the statue erected to that movie reference. He hadn't even grown up here, so the irritation didn't make a lot of sense.

Besides, the incident had happened in the shadow of a different statue grouping entirely. The elaborate Washington Monument sculpture group with its cast of dozens had been witness to Mrs. Weltham's strange behavior and fainting spell. Several witnesses had heard her asking if there was a Ren Faire going on, though she didn't respond to them when they spoke to her. Moments later, she had collapsed at the foot of the monument, directly under the reclining elk.

Vikash wasn't certain what they hoped to find here. Maybe the monument was infested with venomous pill bugs? He was just contemplating the tedium of searching through every crevice of statuary, from the tri-corner hat on George's head to the nooks and crannies of the large North American animals at the bottom, when Kyle nudged him with an elbow, pointing toward one of the reclining moose.

Sitting on the steps beside the moose, feeding the birds from a paper bag, sat a figure from which all the tourists shied away. The leather sleeve dipped into the bag, emerged with the end shut and opened to throw more food to the milling pigeons and sparrows.

"Mr. Jacket!" Vikash called out and raised a hand in welcome.

The familiar animated black leather jacket, which operated as its own being without the help of any human, clutched its bag of birdseed close, shoulders hunched, giving every indication of considering flight. Through whatever mechanism it used to observe the world, though, it obviously recognized them and raised a sleeve to wave back.

"Good to see you, LJ," Kyle said as he sat on one side of the jacket, Vikash on the other. "We were worried about you when you disappeared from the hospital."

The leather shoulders shrugged and one sleeve reached over to pat Vikash's knee.

"It's all right, Mr. Jacket," Vikash said. "Just good to know you're okay."

"Though living a little rough, it looks like." Kyle picked a bit of dried grass from Jacket's collar.

Another shrug and the sleeve not holding the bag described an arc to indicate their surroundings.

"You like outdoors better," Vikash guessed.

The upper half of the jacket bobbed up and down in his version of a nod. Then he pointed a sleeve back and forth between Kyle and Vikash.

"Oh, we've been all right," Kyle said with his easy, beautiful smile. "Investigating something a little weird, but that's no different than any other day, right? Matter of fact, maybe you can help. We know you see all sorts of things we don't."

Jacket made a little rolling 'go on' motion with his sleeve. When Vikash pulled the test tube from his shirt pocket, though, he reared back, yanking his sleeves close in a horrified gesture.

"You know what this is," Vikash prompted.

"Could just be scared of bugs," Kyle muttered.

A hard slap of leather echoed through the oval as Jacket smacked Kyle's arm. Vikash thought his face might fall off, he fought so hard to keep his features still. "Pill bugs are crustaceans, Kyle." He held out the test tube, though farther away from Jacket. "You've seen these?"

Jacket nodded again and shuddered.

"Another officer and I were…" Vikash fought for how to put it. "Injected by these. Vance Virago had a terrifying experience and is still hospitalized. He believed his arm had been bitten off by a prehistoric creature."

For a moment, Jacket was still. Then he began to shake rhythmically, one sleeve making a slapping motion where a knee would be if a person wore him.

"Hey!" Kyle nudged him with his shoulder. "I know you don't like Vance, but it's not funny. Okay. It's a little funny. But not that funny. And Kash was freaked out by what happened to him, too."

Jacket patted the air in a placating gesture. He poked Vikash's arm, then held one sleeve out flat while he made loopy, scribbling motions with the other.

"Oh. Yes, of course." Vikash put the test tube back and carefully removed his pocket notebook and a pen, though he wasn't sure how Jacket would manage without fingers.

He opened the notebook to a blank page and expected to have to hold it, but Jacket closed his right sleeve over the bottom of the notebook and used Vikash's knee as a table of sorts while his left sleeve crimped tight around the pen. The whole operation caused a flutter of excitement in Vikash's chest since he was certain Jacket was going to write a message, to communicate effectively with them for the first time. When Jacket started scribbling meaningless lines on the page, he felt absurdly disappointed.

After a moment, Vikash leaned closer and realized Jacket wasn't writing. He was drawing. A dozen little segmented ovals decorated the bottom half of the page. Jacket tapped them with this pen, then pointed at Vikash's pocket.

"The pill bugs?" Kyle asked.

Jacket nodded and began drawing again, a much larger oval, ten times larger than the small ones. He drew arrows from them to the single, large oval. Vikash gnawed at his bottom lip, trying to make the intuitive leap to understand.

"They came from, like, a mother ship or something?" Kyle ventured.

Jacket shook his head and tapped the page, small ovals to large.

"No." Vikash blinked hard as he caught up to the meaning. "That's Mom. The mother pill bug. The ones we've encountered are...her young?"

With an encouraging shoulder bump, Jacket nodded.

"Holy shit," Kyle muttered. "How big is this thing?"

Another round of drawing on the next page, this time a rectangle on wheels with what looked like a parasol shading it. Jacket drew the mother pill bug beside and roughly the same size as this item.

Kyle's ginger eyebrows drew together as he tried to puzzle it out. "Aw, man. That's a hot dog cart, isn't it? This thing's the size of a freaking hot dog cart?"

"Where have you seen it?" Vikash prompted.

Jacket moved his sleeve slowly from left to right, probably meaning all around. He returned to the page and drew a crescent moon and some messy, five-pointed stars.

"You've seen her different places, but only at night?"

Kyle persisted. "But where? And where is she putting these kids of hers?"

More drawings, hastily rendered, emerged on the next page. Stick figures standing atop rectangles in different poses, one riding what could have been a stick figure horse.

"Statues. She leaves her young only on statues?" Hope and despair warred in Vikash's brain. This would be a clear pattern, but the city contained a horde, a *plague* of sculptures.

Holding the pad and pen out to Vikash, Jacket nodded again, retrieved his bag and hopped down from the step he'd been resting on.

"Thanks for all the help, LJ. We really appreciate it." Kyle held up a hand before Jacket could float away. "One more thing. Why aren't the tourists freaked out by you?"

The rhythmic shaking returned, Jacket's version of laughter. He pointed between himself and the museum.

"Ah." Vikash followed his pointing as a tourist family stopped to snap a photo of Jacket. "They think you're some sort of art installation."

"Got it. You be careful out there, LJ. And be good."

Jacket waved as he floated off toward the park, soon lost from sight behind the museum.

"What's the smile for?" Kyle asked as he got up and dusted off the seat of his uniform pants.

Was I smiling? Oh. "It was good to see him. To see he's all right."

"Yeah. It was. Wonder if there's some way we can get him on payroll?"

Vikash turned that over a moment. He knew Kyle was grateful for Jacket's intervention in their near-fatal confrontation with the giant snapping turtle. He was, too, and he genuinely liked Jacket, but on city payroll? "As an informant?"

"Paranormal community outreach? I don't know, Kash. Just thinking out loud. Something to run by the lieutenant."

"Yes." *I love how your mind works, how you're always thinking of others, even if they're not human. And I can't say that to you here. Why can't I just say it?* "Next site?"

Kyle was giving him an odd look, arms crossed over his chest. "Yeah. No…wait. We should check George and company for pill bugs."

The enormity of that task hit Vikash again, and if they spent the time here instead of trying to find the mother bug… He held up a finger, asking Kyle to wait while he texted Shira.

Did Tim see Weltham? Pill bug confirmed?

After a ten-second delay, Shira sent back to both of them, *Confirmed*.

"We can't just leave the site unsecured," Kyle said as he glanced between his phone and the statue grouping.

No. They couldn't. Another person, or multiple people, might have bugs attach to them. An older individual or someone with medical issues, and they might be looking at a pill bug-related death rather than just dislocation trauma. "Police tape and a call to central dispatch?"

"Sounds like a plan. The city doesn't have enough officers to secure all the damn statues, but we can make sure on the confirmed ones." Kyle planted his feet and pointed with his chin toward the squad car. "I'll stay here and keep people back for now."

Within half an hour, they had the monument cordoned off with police barricade tape and had both city uniforms and park officers there to make sure no one mounted the several sets of steps or climbed onto the statuary of the monument. Counterparts thanked, site secured, Kyle still muttering about Philly having the most statues per square mile, they drove off to their next possible pill bug site by the Academy of Fine Arts. The young man, Max Harrison, had collapsed in the middle of Lenfest Plaza. Unfortunately, this gave them several options to consider and all of them, in theory, might be time-venom pill bug infested.

"We really should have had Tim," Vikash said as they pulled up to the curb.

"Yeah, well, hindsight and all that. It's not like this stuff is covered in any procedural."

The Paint Torch, the Claes Oldenburg giant paintbrush at the entrance to the plaza, was the least likely spot. The sculpture was tall, certainly, but didn't have all the nooks and convenient hiding places the Washington Monument or the Playing Angels hosted. Vikash shielded his eyes with his hand, turning a full circle beside the fifty-foot brush. The Academy itself, a beautifully orchestrated Frank Furness creation that pulled in several schools of design, was liberally peppered, salted and otherwise spiced with sculptural elements. All sorts of places there for Mama Bug to hide her babies. Farther in toward Carlisle Street, where the pedestrian plaza gave way to car traffic again, loomed the Grumman Greenhouse sculpture, an old military plane reshaped and repurposed as a plant nursery.

"She'd like that," he murmured, though Kyle was close enough to hear.

"She? Oh, yeah. I'd guess so. Seems like an ideal playpen for —"

A thunderclap directly in front of them interrupted him, wind rushing out from a squirming, glowing blob at the center of the plaza. The blob resolved briefly into three figures, one multilegged and segmented, the other two human. The humans were trying to hang on to the multilegged creature that thrashed and bucked.

In a tinny, distant voice, one of the humans called out, "Net! Pull it tight!"

The figures vanished in another thunderclap, the air rushing back inward to fill the suddenly empty space.

"Kyle?" Vikash asked in a small voice.

"Yeah?"

"Was that…us?"

"This would be one of those rare times I'd love to say no to you." Kyle swallowed hard. "But, um, yeah. That looked like us."

Chapter Five

Vikash couldn't recall how to move his feet. "That's not possible."

"We can't both hallucinate the same thing, Kash."

"No?"

"It's…" Kyle's ginger eyebrows twisted and pulled together in a puzzled way. "Well, I guess it's possible. But it sounds like a long shot, right?"

Vikash drew in a slow breath. "I like that idea better than us riding a giant crustacean. Time traveling. Or parallel universe hopping or whatever *that*—"

He snapped his mouth shut when his control of pitch and volume slipped. Not the place to make a scene. Not that anywhere in public was a good place, but this… Kyle was already distressed. *Calm. I have to stay calm.*

Kyle paced over to the spot where the strange apparition had popped in and out of view. "Maybe we sh—"

In midword, Kyle vanished. Not just Kyle, the plaza, the street, the *city* vanished.

"Not again," Vikash whispered, though there was no one around to hear.

Pine trees towered over him, old forest giants, with ferns and brambles beginning to poke through what looked like the remnants of a late snow. The shadows cast chill fingers, but the air wasn't bitter. Early spring, he thought, wherever he was. Whenever he was.

Another pill bug must have fallen on him and found skin while he stood in the plaza. Unlike his first time dislocation, he wasn't blindingly terrified. To some extent, he knew what to expect. His body had probably collapsed by now and Kyle would know precisely why. His partner would find the baby pill bug and remove it, and Vikash would wake up in his correct time.

All he had to do was stay relatively safe while he was under the time-venom's influence. While he didn't have any evidence to back up his hunch, he had the oddest feeling that dying here in the hallucination, mental displacement, or whatever this was would mean his body would die in the physical world. A few hours, he just had to stay safe for a few hours.

The surrounding scenery was peaceful enough to give him hope. A huge condor-like raptor circled in the sky to his left. Another, possibly a stork relative, paced through the shallow waters of a nearby pond with grave dignity. Quiet, serene, obviously prehistoric, but late enough along the timeline that birds had replaced dinosaurs. Easy enough to find a rock, sit in the sun and watch the birds while he waited to wake up.

Insect noises crept up through the reeds as he settled on a flat-topped boulder near the pond. At least, Vikash assumed they were insect noises, sleepy peeps and whirs that probably meant things were just waking from winter. A water bug skittered, leaving a miniature wake on the water's calm surface. A strange moth fluttered by in the uneven stock chart gait of all moths, its black wings dotted with blue and red stippling. No moth like it existed in Vikash's Pennsylvania, and a living example of a presumably extinct moth gave him more of a chill than the missing buildings had.

The trees on the other side of the pond gave way to grassland, the brown, swaying stalks showing hints of green near the ground. Animals moved on that sea of brown, horses, though they didn't look quite like horses, and…camels? Really big camels, if that's what they were, or small horses, hard to tell when he was unsure of distance.

Rustling in the undergrowth pulled his gaze in closer, where the passage of something large caused the bushes to wave and shudder. A huge, hooved creature lumbered into the clearing, shaggy and heavy-shouldered like a bison but with the thick brow ridge and horns of a musk ox. It turned toward him, chewing, and Vikash held his breath. He might be able to outrun the beast, but it felt like a sucker's bet.

Dark eyes the size of dinner plates regarded him steadily as if to say, *what are* you *looking at?*

Abruptly, it apparently decided Vikash wasn't a threat and turned its great head away to lumber out into the grass. His heart gave a painful thud before it slid back into a normal rhythm. Maybe he wasn't as safe here as he'd thought.

Megafauna.

The word popped up from somewhere in the swamp of his subconscious. This was the end of the ice age. He couldn't remember the proper term for it, but the receding of the glaciers when huge mammals still roamed North America. Tempting to take pictures, but when he checked, his cell phone had died without a whimper, and they would be hallucinogenic pictures in any case. Or pictures of hallucinations, or nothing at all, come to think of it, since he would be taking pictures firmly stuck *inside* a hallucination.

Trying to parse through the situation was giving him a headache until a distant howl startled him from his tangled thoughts. *Wolf?* There had been terrifyingly large wolves — dire wolves. Were those still living here? Had they ever lived in North America? What other predators were out there?

Vikash suddenly wished he'd been as interested in prehistoric mammals as he'd been enthralled with dinosaurs as a kid.

Human shouts and canine barks joined the occasional howl, moving closer through the trees. Slowly, Vikash stood, trying to track the sound but not attract the attention of any large mammals, regardless of their dietary habits. Breaking twigs and rattling leaves on his right warned him of the approach of something big just before a bull elk with blood running down his flank crashed through into a nearby clearing. The impressive rack of antlers suggested male, but he told himself sternly not to make assumptions and to stop worrying about ridiculous, academic things.

I'm about to be run over by a wounded, hunted elk and I'm worried about gender.

The elk took two bounds into the clearing, then staggered and turned to face his pursuers, blowing and bellowing. More figures crashed through the brush moments later, barking dogs and people carrying weapons. The dogs resembled huskies with elongated heads. *Or wolves.* The humans, men and teenage boys, had black hair like Vikash's own and skin not far off his shade of bronze. At least he wouldn't appear too alien to them.

Snapping and snarling, the dogs harried the elk from all sides, keeping it from bolting for the grasslands. One of the young men raised his spear and hurled it using an atlatl, a wood and bone spear-thrower. Intellectually, Vikash was fascinated that they used such tools so far back in human history. Viscerally, he cringed as the spear pierced the elk's chest, sending the animal rearing and bellowing before it crashed to the ground.

Three of the older men rushed in with clubs, mercifully putting an end to the elk's desperate thrashing. The teenagers called to the dogs, hauling them away from the kill so their fathers and uncles could deal with the carcass, while for their part, the dogs lost interest in dead elk and fixated on something more interesting.

Vikash.

The largest wolf dogs, a silver and white one and a broad-chested, jet-black one, broke from the milling pack and charged toward him. Vikash flicked open his holster in an automatic response, stopping himself before he could draw his sidearm. Dogs. Not wolves. *No shooting dogs.* Especially not ones that belonged to the people with spears and clubs who had finally spotted him. He stepped behind his rock to put something solid between him and the snarling canines even though the top of the rock only came up to his knees.

When one of the youngsters called out, the charging dogs skidded to a stop, whining and pacing in front of the rock while the men not directly involved in butchering the elk eased cautiously toward Vikash. They clutched weapons, but didn't raise them in threat, approaching him in slow steps, spreading out in a half circle around him as one would with a half-wild horse. Curious more than frightened or angry, Vikash hoped.

He spread his arms wide, speaking softly. "I'm just visiting. Not here to invade your hunting grounds."

Of course, they wouldn't understand the words, but he hoped at least to get his intent across. The younger hunters began an animated whispered discussion, the one with thick black hair gleefully escaping its leather thong to flop over his face gesturing at Vikash and patting the top of his own head.

My hat? Carefully, Vikash reached up and removed his uniform hat, setting off a firestorm of whispered conversation that swept over every member of the welcoming committee. Much gesticulating and pointing at heads ensued until Vikash stepped from behind his rock and held his hat out in both hands. The hunting party stilled and returned to focused observation. Vikash wasn't certain whether he was the subject of a prehistoric natural history discussion or a possible enemy yet. At a gesture from one of the older hunters, the wild-haired youngster edged forward. He extended a shaking hand.

Hoping he'd read the situation correctly, Vikash took the last step between them and offered the hat. A rapid cascade of soft words tumbled from Wild-hair's mouth. He touched two fingers to his forehead and took the foreign article of clothing reverently, turning it over and over in his hands before he offered it the man who had asked him to retrieve it.

Eyes wide, the hunting party gathered around to tough the bill and run dirty fingers over the material while Vikash tried not to flinch. He wasn't *really* here and they weren't *really* leaving streaks of dirt on part of his meticulously maintained uniform. Still, a couple of small shudders snuck through while he waited with his hands held in plain sight. Finally, the oldest hunter banged the butt of his spear on the ground and the others retreated a few steps.

"*Lua cha!*" he said, or that was the closest equivalent Vikash's brain could manage.

Vikash shook his head. "I'm sorry. I don't understand."

The old man regarded him with a frown, then muttered something as he turned away to walk back to the elk and the butchering efforts. One of the young men laughed, though he cut off abruptly when Wild-hair kicked him. Several others were speaking at Vikash rapidly, pointing to him then toward the elk carcass as they walked away. Apparently, they expected him to come along, which made a certain amount of sense. One didn't just leave the weird alien person running around one's hunting grounds unsupervised.

While interacting with new people he couldn't talk to wasn't his favorite thing, Vikash reminded himself that humans had survived largely because of a safety in numbers lifestyle. If there were predators lurking nearby, his chances of dying in this time hallucination dropped significantly in the company of other humans.

As Vikash approached, he was struck again by how vivid the hallucination was. As he drew closer, the miasma of body odor and much-worn animal hide hung in a near-visible cloud over the hunters. It hadn't occurred to him in anthropology classes while studying early humans, but Pleistocene people reeked. The dogs that surrounded Vikash with much serious sniffing, having apparently decided that he was an acceptable human, smelled better than the people. At least they weren't as overwhelmingly pungent.

I suppose I'll go nose blind to it eventually. I hope. Though I'd rather wake up, thank you. Any time now, pill bug venom.

Everyone had joined in preparing the elk meat for transport. Wielding knives of stone and horn tools, the hunters had skinned the carcass and were in the process of cutting the meat from the bone to pile on the stretched-out skin. All the superior nonsense about using every piece of the animal appeared to be just that—nonsense, but the hunters were certainly aware of every part. They took the hooves, horns and some of the long bones. The heart, liver and kidneys went in a hide bag the eldest hunter carried. But the rest of the organs and a portion of the meat, they left with the carcass, carefully laid out around the remaining bones.

A gift for the local scavengers? An acknowledgment that they shared the land with other predators? An offering to a protective spirit or god? Impossible to say. It could have been a notion cooked up by an unbalanced mind. Maybe someone believed that zombie elk ghouls would come and kill everyone in their sleep if they didn't lay these particular parts out in this pattern and had argued convincingly enough that now everyone was terrified of zombie elk ghouls.

And here's where Kyle would tell me how my brain is tilted sideways. Damn it, I want Kyle here. No, that's not right. Not here. I want to be back where Kyle is.

Efficiently and quietly, the hunters finished with astounding speed, partly out of long practice and partly because they divided the labor so well. They tied the lion's share of the meat in the hide and suspended it from a stout branch used as a carry pole. Without another word, they set off at a pace designed to exhaust a marathon runner. Vikash kept up as well as he could, trying to keep to the game trails they took, losing the trail more often than not and crashing through the underbrush. The dogs, and sometimes Wild-hair, kept doubling back for him, herding him in the right direction.

Good thing, since the hunters moved so quietly, he would have lost them in the first five minutes on his own.

He was gasping for air, bent over with his hands braced on his knees, by the time they reached a settlement beside a rushing creek. The wolf dogs surrounded him again, nudging and whining. This obviously wasn't correct behavior for a human.

"I'm all right," he gasped out to dogs who understood him as well as the humans did, which was of course not at all.

If he was going to be shanghaied into these hallucinations, why didn't they come with time-appropriate adaptations or superpowers or some ability to upgrade like a video game?

Women and the children too young to hunt had swarmed the hunters, both in greeting and to take charge of the bounty from the day's stalking. While it was impossible to say if this was a patriarchal society yet, there was obviously a clear division of labor along gender lines. Though why Vikash's brain kept insisting on a return to college anthropology was beyond him.

He did his best to straighten up and appear only mildly winded when the white-haired eldest hunter pointed to him, speaking in rapid, clipped sentences. The entire group of women and every child over the age of three turned with solemn frowns to regard him where he stood on the rise leading into the settlement. An older woman, who seemed to be Eldest Hunter's counterpart, had a rapid, sharp exchange with the men. Then she made an odd tilt-tilt gesture with her head and flapped her hands at some of the youngsters gathered in clumps. The clumps scattered on her command, most of children peeling off to help various adults, while one group of perhaps ten to twelve year olds scampered up the hill to Vikash. They shoved right through the still-circling wolf dogs to grab his hands and pull him down toward the center of the settlement. No hesitation, no fear — Vikash had either been judged completely harmless by the adults or these youngsters had never encountered another human who meant them harm.

Wide-eyed kids pawed at his clothes, exclaiming over the material. Tunics and leggings predominated in both children and adults, loose garments sewn with careful rawhide stitches. While the hides were crudely cured and often still had the hair or fur on the outsides, a far cry from the smooth, machine-stitched clothes Vikash wore, their garments were also nothing like the ridiculous one-shoulder fur sacks modern people thought of as prehistoric attire, Raquel Welch in *One Million Years B.C.* notwithstanding.

When he reached Eldest Mother, she looked him up and down, fingering his jacket, her mouth set in a hard line. Her dark eyes held questions Vikash couldn't hope to answer, but she quickly buried wonder under practicality as she began issuing instructions again.

A little girl ran up to offer Vikash some water in a rough wooden bowl, and he tried not to think about the bacteria and parasites squirming in it. He wasn't really drinking it, after all, and his hallucinatory self was thirsty. Then the kids led him through the wood and grass huts to a bend in the creek where deposited gravel and sand had created a little beach.

The kids chattered and milled about, occasionally trying to drag Vikash into conversation. One little girl took off her little boot-shoes and waded out into the creek, which had to be freezing, while one of the youngest kept bringing shiny stones for Vikash to admire. Typical kids. Funny how that didn't change.

Just as he started wondering why they'd brought him to the creek, Wild-hair bounded down the embankment with a huge grin and two spears. His teeth were surprisingly good for someone with no acquaintance with toothpaste or fluoride, but he probably didn't eat much sugar, either. He began chattering the moment he was in earshot, an irrepressible presence, almost as if his quieter, more serious elders had poured all of their optimism and *joie de vivre* into him for safekeeping. He gestured the children back and to Vikash's astonishment, they obeyed immediately, settling wide-eyed and without argument on various logs and rocks farther up the embankment.

Still chatting away, Wild-hair handed Vikash one of the spears with its atlatl. Vikash startled when Wild-hair patted his hip, but there seemed nothing suggestive or intimate in the gesture, just a friendly nudge. His shooing motions indicated Vikash was supposed to move aside. With his bright smile still firmly in place, Wild-hair pushed the errant lock of hair from his face, pointed to a log upstream, and hurled his spear.

The missile hit with a solid *thunk*, the haft quivering from the force of the blow. Wild-hair laughed and said something that might as well have been *ta-da!*

"That was amazing. At least thirty yards." Vikash offered a bit of a smile in return, hoping that his words sounded approving, at least.

To Vikash's horror, Wild-hair pointed to the spear in Vikash's hand and to the log. His meaning was quite clear. He wanted to see Vikash throw, and while he might understand using an atlatl in theory, Vikash had no idea how to put it into practice. *The butt end of the spear fits into the hooked end of the thrower. Arm back. Hold it straight. And...*

Despite putting the full force of his arm behind the throw, the spear ended up in the sand three feet in front of Vikash. A strangled sound came from Wild-hair and, yes, when Vikash checked, his face had that fighting-a-laugh contortion to it. The kids weren't nearly so polite, rolling with helpless giggles.

Wild-hair stroked Vikash's shoulder in a way that would've been far too familiar in his own time, but here...here the kids piled over one another like puppies. It felt more usual and normal than invasive. With a lot more patient chattering, Wild-hair demonstrated how he held the atlatl, how the spear ran parallel to his arm and how he snapped the atlatl forward on the throw. Then he pointed, indicating that Vikash should try again.

I can do this. Vikash had never been a star athlete, nothing like that, but he had been competent on the soccer field and not terrible on the track. He pulled his arm back, let out a slow breath and hurled the spear as hard as muscle and sinew allowed.

The spear buried itself halfway up the shaft in the sand near his feet.

Wild-hair murmured softly as he retrieved both spears, the disappointment in his tone obvious, but sympathy seemed to creep in, too. He looped an arm around Vikash's waist to turn him and start him back toward the settlement, still talking as they walked. The kids bounced and raced about them like tiny, overenthusiastic satellites, asking questions, all of which Wild-hair answered with patient good humor.

More question and answer followed when they rejoined the adults. Eldest Mother's frown deepened while Eldest Hunter made some gesture that might have meant *oh well, it was too much to hope that he might be useful*. Or it might have meant *go away, kid, you bother me*. When even the body language was foreign, it was tricky to get a foothold in the linguistic cliff.

Wild-hair startled Vikash with a hard hug and got him settled on a log not far from the cook fire, one of the best vantage points to take in the efficient bustle of the settlement preparing for nightfall. Men and women worked together on the elk meat, hanging strips on a rack to dry, dumping chunks into the water contained in a hollowed-out center of a large stone set in the middle of the fire. The older children dragged piles of brush and thorn into place around the settlement as a makeshift fence, most likely against large predators.

In the midst of feeling useless, Vikash gleaned bits and pieces of social cues and structures. The kids were an indistinguishable pack for the most part. None of them answered to any one adult in particular that he could make out, and all of the adults directed their energies and corrected bad behavior. Something Vikash was used to in an extended family situation, which this could have been, where the kids were everyone's kids.

But the young adults gave him pause.

Everyone touched as a normal, natural part of communication. Hair, hands, shoulders, arms, and hips were all fair game. More intimate touching, close embraces, suggestive caresses, happened right out in public too, but not with everyone.

Eldest Hunter nuzzled at the nape of Eldest Mother's neck. She swatted at him, laughing. Two of the older women kissed in a more than friendly way before separating to complete chores. The adults had partners and they declared their allegiances without shame, regardless of gender pairings.

The younger adults? They defied every social structure in Vikash's experience. Wild-hair snagged a young man as he walked past, one whose limping gait caused him to stumble into Wild-hair's embrace. They both laughed softly as they nuzzled each other's throats and rocked their groins together. Vikash yanked his head around to stare at his boots, his face fever-hot and tight, though he kept stealing sideways glances. They were so open about wanting each other and no one shouted invective at them or even shot a single evil glance their way.

Without missing a thrust, Limpy stuck out a hand and snagged a young woman with a claw necklace as she ambled past. She shrieked and Vikash was certain things would turn ugly, but the yelp of surprise turned into a laugh and all three of them tumbled to a rush mat in front of the largest shelter. What had appeared to be a same-sex couple having public sex turned into a rolling, giggling threesome, then a quartet when another young woman wriggled her way into the groping, humping mass of limbs.

So mortified he wanted to sink into the dirt, but so fascinated he couldn't look away, Vikash stared in astonishment as another and another and another young person joined them. The orgy—anything over three people was an orgy, wasn't it?—eventually swallowed everyone in the settlement under the age of twenty-five. Claw-necklace had mounted Limpy, who had turned his head to suck Wild-hair's cock. No inhibitions, no apparent pressure to adhere to strict boxes of sexuality, they all simply did as they pleased, obviously completely normal for them since the older folks went about their work with a smile or two for the youngsters, and the kids just went about their kid business.

Anger began to curl through the embarrassment in Vikash's gut. Not anger at the settlement's young people, not exactly, but a slow, burning seethe of jealous indignation wormed its way into his normally reasonable thoughts. They could be touch each other openly, regardless of gender, engage in shameless exhibitionism without looking over their shoulders to see who was watching, without fear of someone spewing hateful threats at them or assaulting them with worse than words.

Yes, he recognized that the purpose of the joyful sexual free-for-all in front of him was procreation. But even past child-bearing age, when pairings among these people appeared to take on deeper emotional meaning, he didn't see anyone condemn another's love. He wanted that acceptance in his own time. His trip to the future had shown him a world free of gender and sexuality prejudices. Now his trip to the past snatched up the intolerance of his own time and shoved it in his face. Humans hadn't always drawn such clear, isolating moral boxes, at least not every society.

The human race had taken huge steps backward and mired itself in divisiveness and hate when they could have had…this. All along.

He could have had Kyle all along, openly, without reservation, instead of breaking his heart in slow motion with a thousand tiny ice pick blows every time Vikash flinched or backed away. *I can't keep doing this to him. I can't keep hurting him like this.* The thought only made that black worm of anger grow and gnaw at his insides until his throat felt raw and constricted and his vision blurred with tears. Because he would never have what they shared here. He would never live in a world that could accept all of him instead of picking and choosing the pieces it wanted. But it was still home and Kyle was still there, not here in this dream place. He'd almost begun to doubt any time travel involvement with the pill bug venom until he'd seen himself and Kyle riding the back of the mother pill bug.

It would have been so easy to dismiss his time displacements as wishful thinking, his brain creating worlds he liked better than his own. Difficult to say which was worse, though, a world where societies like this one and future Philadelphia had never and would never exist, or the fact that they had and would, but not for him.

Why am I still here? Why haven't I gotten back to Kyle yet? It's been hours here. Last time, he'd been in the future world maybe two hours at most, and out in the real world over three times that. Kyle must have found the pill bug on him and removed it in a matter of minutes. Following that pattern, this time displacement should have been shorter, with lower levels of venom.

But I'm still here.

Vikash startled out of his thoughts when someone patted him on the shoulder. Eldest Mother stood beside him holding out a thumb-high stack of meat on a little wooden tray. She smiled when he took it and as she shuffled away, he realized the orgy was over. Either he'd zoned out for a long time or it had been the quickest orgy in history. *Flash mob orgy.*

Everyone had wandered away from the site of mass bonking to settle around the cook fire except Wild-hair and Limpy, who still lay tangled in each other's arms, snoring.

The boiled elk was tough and gamey. A pinch of salt or even a little basil or a single cardamom pod would have helped it limp along toward respectable food, and Vikash vowed never to take the spices in his kitchen for granted again. When he got home, he would pull them down from his cabinet, savor their scents and thank them for being in his life. He couldn't offend his hosts, though, so he ate with the rest of the settlement around the cook fire.

Woven bowls of berries were also passed hand to hand to round out the meal and Vikash conceded that those were quite tasty. When everyone retired to the hut shelters, he understood why the elder folks had allowed Wild-hair and Limpy to nap through dinner. They took up spears, wrapped themselves in rough blankets and settled with their backs to the banked coals of the cook fires, peering out into the night. Of course. The Pleistocene was full of dangerous beasts and someone needed to keep watch.

They look good together, those two. I hope they grow old together. I wish... Vikash sliced off that thought before it could grow as he settled down in the musty, sweat-reeking furs with some of the older kids. He was going to go to sleep and wake up in his own time where attitudes were as he had left them. Wishing would get him nowhere. He'd just have to deal with the world as it was.

He drifted off in fits and starts, Kyle's worried face featuring prominently in his hurried snatches of dreams.

* * * *

Sunlight tinged the insides of Vikash's eyelids. He struggled to wake, expecting hospital sheets and antiseptic smells. A deep breath brought him strong body odor and grass.

What the hell?

He scrambled upright before his eyes were fully focused and hit his head on a support branch. The Pleistocene settlement still surrounded him. Why was he still here? He was supposed to be *back* now.

"No," he whispered, sitting down with a thump. "No, no, no."

Maybe it was a cumulative venom effect, but he was still stuck in the past. Going to sleep hadn't solved anything. It might be that nothing would wake him. His heart thudded hard as panic dug icy needles into his chest. He wasn't going to make it home this time.

The young people sharing the shelter with him were scooting away with sideways glances. One of the older girls actually fled the shelter and Vikash forced a deep breath into his lungs. He was scaring the kids.

Wild-hair arrived within seconds, shooed the kids out and took Vikash in his arms. His meaningless words still soothed Vikash's frayed nerves and he finished pulling himself together. Whether he would wake in the correct time that day, the next or never again, he still had to deal with what was in front of him in a calm, sensible way.

Calm. Yes. At least the face he showed the world, as it had always been. His features slipped back into his customary placidness, what Kyle called his statue face. *Stop. No worrying about Kyle right now. Just try to make yourself useful.*

Being useful to a prehistoric community proved harder than Vikash could have imagined. The adult males gathered up weapons and snares to go out for the day's hunting—and Wild-hair made it clear that Vikash wasn't to go with them. Eldest Mother sat Vikash down with her to try to show him how to weave the simple baskets the older children made. His fingers were suddenly so clumsy he couldn't even begin. Claw-necklace set him to grinding rough grains in a stone bowl, but apparently he sucked at that too since she soon took the stone pounder away.

Two of the older women took pity on Vikash, whose humiliation threatened to melt him into a messy globular puddle, and handed him a basket. He was puzzled until the mid-age children, the tribe of perhaps five to eight year olds, tugged him toward the woods and a patch of berry bushes. Good. He could pick berries with the kids and watch out for them. Being an adult male was overrated, anyway.

Still, he proceeded carefully, watching the little ones expertly picking only the deepest purple berries. Only when he was certain he wouldn't also screw up berry picking, he started filling his basket methodically, plucking the berries the little ones couldn't reach. The day was warm enough, though his fingers were chilled, and the kids around him chattered happily to him, not at all bothered when he couldn't answer them.

His continued presence in this time still bothered him, but the berry picking pushed the anxious gnawing further back in his brain. The sun warmed the back of his jacket and he had nearly fooled himself into a contented state when the little ones directly beside him stiffened, quivering in their heightened alertness. Vikash went down on one knee, searching on the patch of undergrowth on which the kids fixated. *There*. Something large enough to shake branches crept through the brush.

Vikash handed off his basket to one of the boys and motioned the kids behind him. Silently, they backed away as a group from whatever creature threatened them, the most basic primal understanding taking the place of verbal communication. A second rustling started to the left of the first. They were being stalked.

Carefully, never taking his eyes from the shivering leaves, Vikash bent to pick up a heavy branch. He made running motions with his fingers, hoping the kids got it. Whatever these things were, he was going to do his best to give the kids a chance to get back to the settlement and relative safety.

The first animal shoved its head through the leaves and Vikash nearly dropped his branch. It held its broad feline head low between powerful shoulders, thick legs more reminiscent of bear than cat stalking cautiously forward. Roughly the size of a lion, it could have been a mutant cougar except for the curved dagger canines protruding from its upper jaw. Longer than the biggest knife in Vikash's kitchen, there would be no pulling away if those teeth sank into him.

Smilodon. Saber tooth. Seeing them in natural history displays didn't do justice to their panic-inducing size. A deep growl rumbled in the cat's chest, breaking Vikash's paralysis. He waved the kids on, yelling, "Run! Go!" The words might not have parsed, but his meaning couldn't have been any clearer. The kid herd stampeded back toward the settlement just as two more huge cats broke cover.

Kids in Vikash's time would have run in a screaming mob and saber-tooth take the hindmost. The prehistoric kids ran in eerie silence, as a herd, the bigger ones scooping up the little ones who lagged. Incredibly smart, since big cats often needed to be able to pick an individual target, and the silence allowed Vikash to become the center of attention.

"Hey! Big ugly orthodontally challenged kitty cats!" he bellowed, waving his branch club in wild arcs.

"Over here! You don't want the little ones! Here! Bigger meat!"

The largest smilodon turned toward him, crouched and snarling. The other ones still focused on the kids. Rage and panic collided, skittering across Vikash's nerves. He leaped forward and smacked the one closest to him in the shoulder. An incredibly stupid move, but the damn predators weren't getting kids for lunch.

Vikash risked a glance to his left. The third cat still prowled after the children while the first two circled to cut him off from the settlement. Damn cats. Couldn't go after the armed adults. No. They knew better, coming after people too small to hold a spear.

His anger sparked in fretful bursts, catching on the tinder of weeks of anxiety. The cat trying to get around him to the kids bounded forward and Vikash's rage ignited, arc-welder bright in his head as it leaped from him. A dry branch crackled overhead and snapped, plummeting in a shower of leaves and twigs to smack the cat between the shoulders. It shrieked in shock and reversed course.

Now Vikash found himself the focus of three sets of feline eyes. He gripped his impromptu club tight, swinging it in whistling arcs to keep the cats back.

That's it. Eyes on me. But what the hell am... Gun. You have a real weapon, you idiot.

Slowly he unsnapped his holster and drew out his sidearm, trying to keep all three cats in sight as they crouched low and snarling, ears flattened, upper lips pulled back to expose the full length of saber canines.

Branch down. Two-handed grip.

The largest cat let out a scream that sent all Vikash's calm running for the exits. He swung toward it instinctively and the cat on his left leaped at him. Two shots rang in his ears before three hundred pounds of monster cat slammed into him, claws raking his chest. He managed one more shot before they collided with the ground. Between the force of the blow and the cat's weight, Vikash fought for breath. His sight darkened along the edges. He was going to die now, here on prehistoric grass, while his body died back in Lenfest Plaza. A sense of peace tinged with bitterness rolled over him as the world went away.

At least the kids are safe. I'm so damn sorry, Kyle.

* * * *

His eyes flew open on an agonized gasp. The light was wrong. The shadows larger. The weight had vanished from his chest. Where were the cats? Where was his gun? Vikash surged up with a wild cry, searching surroundings he couldn't place.

"Hey, hey! Easy, big guy." Kyle's voice. *Kyle. Holy mother of gods.*

Familiar scarred hands gripped Vikash's shoulders. Kyle's smile, the worried crinkling of his forehead, Lenfest Plaza.

"How long?"

"Easy, Kash. You're okay. Ambulance is coming."

Vikash seized Kyle's jacket in both hands, his voice far too shaken and ferocious as he demanded, "*How long was I out?*"

"About fifteen minutes." Kyle's smile slid sideways. "I got the little bugger off you just a couple seconds after you went down. Was it a bad one this time?"

"It was... I was..." Vikash loosened his grip, feeling lost and dizzy. "Fifteen minutes?"

"Yeah." Kyle drew the word out, obviously turning things over. "How long did you think you were gone?"

Vikash shook his head. He understood the question, but he didn't feel steady enough to answer. A day and night in his time displacement, but only a few minutes for his physical self? What did that mean?

One of Kyle's hands still gripped his shoulder. He looked so worried. Vikash struggled to say something. "I hope the kids are okay."

"Um, I hope so, too?" Kyle pointed to the street. "It's fine. I know you'll explain later. EMTs are here, so for right now, just, you know, breathe."

"No."

"No what? Kash, talk to me, for fuck's sake."

Vikash pulled out of Kyle's grip and fought to get his feet under him. "No hospital." He put a hand on the wall beside him to steady himself. "No ambulance. I'm fine."

"Like hell you are," Kyle said softly. "You're about as far from fine as I am from tall. But no one's gonna force you to go."

His chest hurt. It shouldn't have. His head, yes, since he'd probably hit it when he'd fallen. Half-turned away from Kyle, he undid the top buttons of his uniform shirt. Several faint scratches scored his chest.

"Kyle?" he whispered as he rebuttoned with shaking hands.

"Yeah? Kash, you've gone kinda gray."

"Was I *here*? The whole time?"

He expected Kyle to ask him what he meant or say something sarcastic. His partner's silence made him whirl around to find Kyle staring at the ground, obviously searching for words.

"You...you kinda wavered for a couple seconds." Kyle swallowed hard. "I know that doesn't make any sense. You didn't vanish or anything. But you weren't as *solid*, for just about long enough for me to panic. It was fucking weird."

Vikash patted his shoulder, wishing for perhaps the hundredth time that week that he could pull Kyle close and hold him to ease the anguish and confusion in those green eyes. But a crowd had gathered and the EMTs were hurrying toward them.

The overwhelming feeling of *not here, not now* nearly made him scream, but he tucked his hands under his armpits instead of reaching for Kyle.

In that moment of disoriented misery, a thought took root. "Kyle? It was bigger, wasn't it?"

"The pill bug?" Kyle pulled a test tube out of his inside jacket pocket with the safely contained pill bug. "I'd have to measure, but I think so."

Vikash nodded as Kyle stepped away to run interference with the medics. The little ones were growing, and their time-traveling abilities growing with them. The shakes clawed up from his gut when a horrible thought ambushed him. A permanent home in the Pleistocene had been far too close. With a pill bug who was another day or two older, Vikash might well have been actual smilodon lunch.

Chapter Six

Late afternoon sun filtered through the back windows of the squad room when all the officers of the 77th reconvened. Vikash sat shivering with a mug of tea clutched in both hands. He couldn't get warm, even huddled in his heavy winter jacket.

"Soren!" Lieutenant Dunfee's voice sliced through the room. "Do we need to get you back to the hospital?"

He shook his head, knew that wouldn't be enough for her and forced out, "No, ma'am. I'm all right."

All three reported patients had been in possession of pill bug hitchhikers. All three were recovering, with better results than poor Vance, with their parasites in custody. Known sites had been secured to protect the public, there had been no sighting of the mother bug besides the disturbing vision in Lenfest Plaza, and Vikash had no idea what to suggest next if someone asked. At least they could make the educated guess that the amount of venom injected correlated directly to the length of the mental time dislocation, but that didn't resolve much of anything. With the pill bugs growing, they grew more dangerous, and there was no way to know how many babies the mother bug had seeded throughout the city or how many *more* young she could have if they didn't catch her.

Tim rolled up to his desk and wriggled out of his paper conveyance, crooning at him in a sympathetic way that let Vikash know he must have looked terrible.

"All right, people." Lieutenant Dunfee shook her head. "I have two officers on medical, one close to collapse and the rest of you look like crap."

"Well, thank you for that." Carrington sniffed in offense from his corner.

"If we try to solve this tonight, we're asking for disaster. Everyone get the hell out of my building. We'll start again in the morning." She pointed toward the shadowed back wall. "Except Loveless, who wants to be a smartass. Go find that damn jacket. Get him to agree to come in tomorrow morning. We'll pay him out of outreach, since we never touch those funds. Or feed him. Or give him a place to sleep. I don't know! Whatever the hell an animated jacket wants."

"*Oui, mon général.*" Carrington saluted from his corner.

"Wrong pronoun. Just get out there." The lieutenant was still shaking her head as she strode back to her office, muttering, "Smartass vampire."

The scraping of chairs and shuffling of belongings followed as everyone got ready to leave.

"I'll drive you," Kyle said as he stood and reached for Vikash's shoulder.

Vikash twitched away. *Not here. Not in front of everyone*. The moment he did it, he recognized it as a particularly stupid mistake. Putting a hand on a shaken partner's shoulder wasn't anything an observer would misunderstand. His overreaction had probably looked stranger than anything Kyle would have done, and now the hurt was all too obvious in Kyle's eyes.

There should have been something he could have said, but Kyle had already turned away with a falsely cheerful, "Come on. Let's get you home."

They made the drive through the city and across the Schuylkill in silence. Vikash didn't know what to say since he didn't have anything to offer Kyle to make it right. He wanted to blurt out everything about the prehistoric people and the wonderfully, embarrassingly open society they had, but that probably would've made things worse. For his part, Kyle simply drove, eyes forward, jaw tight. Instead of pulling into the parking lot at Vikash's apartment, he stopped at the curb out front.

"Aren't—" Vikash had to clear the squeak from his throat. "Not coming up?"

"Don't think so. You need to rest." Kyle sounded reasonable and calm, but he wouldn't meet Vikash's gaze. "I'll see you in the morning."

"All right." With those two words, Vikash was certain he was nailing the last board over their relationship. His feet moved without him asking. He managed, lead-limbed and aching, to climb out of Kyle's car, one of the hardest things he had ever forced himself to do.

Kyle drove off without another word, without even a wave, leaving Vikash staring after the accusatory red glow of his taillights. *It's better this way. Kyle needs someone he can have a real relationship with, not someone who needs to hide him. He doesn't deserve to be anyone's dirty little secret. He deserves so much more.*

Vikash wondered if his chest might break open and spill all the bitter acid of those thoughts onto the sidewalk. The pain rode so heavy around his heart that his rib cage couldn't possibly contain it. He wanted to hold hands in a restaurant, wanted to accept the little bits of discreet affection Kyle offered in public. He wanted to go home to his parents and say, "This is my boyfriend, Kyle."

He wanted to tell Kyle he loved him.

But he'd always had issues with getting all of his thoughts to form useful words, especially when they weren't nice, clean, factual thoughts. Even if he could have spoken easily, he couldn't say those things to Kyle. How could he saddle Kyle with someone who couldn't give him all he needed? Better to let him go. Let him find someone good for him, someone who made him laugh, smile, and didn't twitch every time Kyle got too close in public.

His steps echoed, sharp and hollow, as he climbed to his second-floor apartment. While he managed to feed Ellie, he didn't have the energy or the appetite for dinner himself. Curled up on the sofa, still fully dressed, he acknowledged his cowardice. The time travel event, that glimpse of them with the mother pill bug, had scared the hell out of him. He could only assume it was a future event and that, along with his body nearly being kidnapped to the past, frightened him to the point of his brain nearly shutting down. Kyle hadn't reacted badly to seeing himself bull-riding a giant bug, though he had to know what it meant.

That unwavering courage made everything harder, made Vikash ashamed of how he avoided things he had to face. Ellie mewed and jumped onto the sofa to curl up in the crook of Vikash's arm. He petted her absently, letting her purr motor soothe him. He had two choices if he didn't want to hurt Kyle long-term. He could try to be more relaxed and open about their relationship—which wasn't going to happen, it never had — or he could tell Kyle in the gentlest terms that it was over. *It's not you. It's me.*

Except in this case, it really was.

Tomorrow after shift, that's when he would do it. For Kyle's sake, for his happiness, he had to end it before things went too far. They could work together and be good friends, he was sure of it. But he couldn't keep clinging to Kyle when his partner needed more. Time for all that tomorrow.

* * * *

Sunlight prodded at Vikash the next morning and he jerked off the sofa, sending Ellie scampering in a white puff of irritated fur. He'd overslept and didn't have time for much more than a quick shave and a change from the uniform he'd slept in to a fresh, pressed one from the closet. He groaned when he realized his car was at the station and he would have to navigate SEPTA to get to work.

On the coffee table, his phone chirped a text alert. Kyle.

U coming?

Vikash sighed and texted back.

Might be late. Catching the bus.

Kyle sent an emoji rolling its eyes.

I'm downstairs, dumbass.

Oh. He hadn't expected a ride, since Kyle's apartment was much closer to work and he'd have to drive across the river, then double back. Typical Kyle, going out of his way to help. Vikash stuck the phone in his pocket, fed Ellie, then yanked his jacket on as he raced down the stairs.

"Hey! Feel better this morning?" Kyle offered a tentative smile and a white paper bag.

"Some. What's this?"

"Takeout from Green Eggs. Got you the smoked lox omelet. You haven't been eating enough."

"Ah. Thank you." Vikash kept it on his lap. Easier to eat when they got to the squad room. "And you?"

"Ultimate tofu, baby! You know I have to have it."

A smile twitched at Vikash's lips even though he didn't feel at all like smiling. It was so hard to stay depressed around Kyle. The silence between them was better than it had been the previous evening, less strained.

When they entered the squad room, a black shape swooped across the room at Vikash. He nearly panicked and ducked, his thundering heart insisting an attack was in progress, but the shape resolved into Leather Jacket, who hugged Vikash tightly before abandoning him to embrace Kyle as well.

"All right, people, let's settle." Lieutenant Dunfee tapped an old-fashioned wooden pointer against the whiteboard. "Ladies and gentlemen and nonhuman…consultants, we're dispensing with roll call this morning in favor of a war council."

Vikash hurried to his seat, and since most of his squad mates were scarfing down breakfast, he pulled the Styrofoam containers out of the bag, checked to make sure he gave Kyle the right one and dug in. *Oh, that's so good.* Eggs and fish might not have appealed to some people, but for him, this was the perfect breakfast and hit his sugar-crashed body with just the right kick. *So much better than gamey, unseasoned elk meat.*

He shot Kyle a grateful look before turning his body toward the lieutenant and the whiteboard.

"Primary target today is Mama Pill Bug. You've all seen her young, but I believe only Mr. Jacket has had a clear visual on mom."

Jacket gave her his version of a nod, while beside him, Tim reared up from his paper sphere and squeaked. He wore something blue on what was presumably his head. Someone had made him a tiny police hat?

"And possibly Tim has, as well. That said, Mr. Jacket has been generous enough to donate his time to help us locate said giant crustacean, from his description identical to the pill bugs we have in custody but about the size of a street vendor's cart."

"Giant snapping turtles, giant freaking bugs," Wolf grumbled. "What's next, giant killer shrews?"

"Oh my God, Wolf, shush!" Shira waved her hands in negation as office supplies flew off her desk in graceful swan dives to the floor. "You don't *say* things like that around here!"

"Focus, people," the lieutenant admonished. "Officers will take their regular assigned patrol routes. I'll coordinate from here. Mr. Jacket will take Tim and go hunting, but if any of you come across suspected pill bug-related incidents or disturbances first, call in immediately. Mr. Jacket will have a cell so I can send him to you as needed. Containment, everyone. Let's not have a repeat of the incident with Tim's stick house."

Tim's sad peep underscored that warning. One could only imagine how much work that branch and twig ball had been for him to build.

"And this is one SPU will want to get their hands on. Questions? Good. Normal patrol schedules. Don't rush out there. Give Mr. Jacket some time for reconnaissance. LJ, my office. I'll get you set with a phone."

LJ? Lieutenant Dunfee was on an initials-only basis with Leather Jacket? "Just when you thought the world was out of surprises."

"Hmm?" Kyle asked around a bite of breakfast.

"Mumbling out loud." Vikash shoveled down the rest of his food to avoid looking at Kyle too long. *Say it. Ask if he's free tonight. That you need to talk.* But nothing made it past his swiftly closing throat.

When they went out back to the squad car, they walked around to their accustomed doors. Kyle always drove and Vikash never challenged him unless Kyle wasn't at his best, physically, which was rare. He didn't mind. It gave him time to think, sometimes to turn over the particulars of a case. Besides, Kyle was the native and knew the streets better than any GPS ever would.

Most days, the thinking time was a good thing.

"Kyle?"

"I'm right here, you know. And haven't forgotten my name yet."

Vikash couldn't muster the snicker that comment should have warranted. "Do you... Can we have dinner? Tonight?"

Kyle gave him an odd sideways glance. "You don't normally ask. You tell me what's for dinner and I show up. What's going on, Kash?"

"Talk. We need to."

"Yeah." Kyle heaved a slow breath. "I kinda guess we do. Couldn't just do it now, huh?"

Vikash shook his head. "This isn't a...work kind of talk."

"Of course it's not," Kyle said softly. "All right. Work. Concentrating on work now. We'll talk tonight."

"Kyle, I'm s—"

A squawk from the radio cut him off. Greg Santos' voice came over their department frequency. "Ma'am, Jacket might want to come down here to FDR Park."

"Based on what, Santos?"

"The ducks, ma'am. They're real upset about something and it doesn't feel like a normal duck being upset something."

"Very specific, Santos. Thank you," Lieutenant Dunfee said at her driest.

"Sorry, ma'am. It's hard to put into human. But the ducks are upset about something and it feels like a really scared, we've-never-seen-this-before kind of upset. The ones at the gazebo by the lake here."

It was the first time Vikash had experienced Greg's particular talent being useful. He heard emotions, but only negative ones and only avian ones, and not just any birds, but only waterfowl. It was one of the most absurdly specific paranormal talents Vikash had ever come across.

"All right. Jacket's on the Broad Street line, heading south. He might have known about that as a possible overnight spot. Zacchini, Loveless, you're closest. Intercept Jacket and Tim at the Race-Vine station. Take them down to FDR."

"Unit Five, copy," Carrington's voice came over the radio, all business now. "On our way."

"All other units, remain on your current routes."

Vikash called in their acknowledgment, *all other* consisting only of him and Kyle, and Wolf and Krisk. Minutes ticked by as Kyle took them slowly through their section of the city, every crackle of the radio zipping across Vikash's nerves. When he realized he was leaning forward, tensed and ready like a foxhound on a short leash, he forced himself to lean back and relax.

The distortion of the radio couldn't hide the extra crispness in Lieutenant Dunfee's voice when she called in next. Something had happened. "Prints confirmed, FDR Park. Jacket and Tim pursuing on foot."

A few minutes passed. Kyle turned onto Race Street.

"All units converge on the City Hall Station. Bug is on the Broad Street local, heading north. Jacket will attempt to force disembarkation."

"Lieutenant, say again?" Carrington's voice came through strained. "She took the train?"

"On the roof. I repeat, all units converge on City Hall Station."

Kyle took a hard right at the next block and turned on the flashers while Vikash called in their location. Traffic was never light in this part of town, but midmorning on a weekday wasn't bad. Most of the office drones were at their desks and few tourists came out on a Tuesday in February.

"Kash, check the schedule," Kyle said as he fought a small patch of ice and careened onto Broad Street.

"Hits the City Hall station at ten-nineteen."

"Five minutes. We're closest in. Nets?"

"In the trunk."

"Good. When we stop, I'll grab them, you start scanning for LJ."

The familiar pattern settled Vikash and helped him focus. His eyes were better and he had the advantage of height, so using him as a spotter instead of Kyle just made sense. He had his door open and his foot on the curb the moment the car stopped rolling. The station itself was underneath City Hall with exits onto the street. If Jacket managed to chase Mama Bug up the stairs, which seemed unlikely, they'd come up on the east side of City Hall with a lot of commotion.

Vikash glanced at his watch. Three minutes. The boulevard was free of panicked citizens. He sent a silent salute to Billy Penn up at the top of the building, took a folded net from Kyle and ran for the subway entrance. Amanda and Carrington arrived in a shriek of tires and brake pads, repeating the motions of net retrieval and vicinity scan.

"Up or down, Carr?" Kyle called out.

"We'll go down," Carrington shouted back, which only made sense. He would be more effective out of the sunlight. "If we can't secure the bug immediately, we'll do our best to herd it up the stairs."

Kyle gave him a nod. "Good. Fighting monsters on a crowded platform sounds like a really bad idea."

"One monster, you wuss," Amanda muttered as she brushed past and hurried down the steps with Carrington close behind.

The train rumbled beneath the street, right on time, screeching in complaint as it slowed to line up with the platform. Voices floated up as people left the cars, laughter, one-sided cell phone conversations, a baby crying. Carrington's voice cut through the background noise, his upper crust, patrician cadence lending authority to his words.

"Ladies and gentlemen, please move to the exit as quickly as possible. We have a police emergency. Please leave the plat—"

Screams cut off his reasonable crowd herding—the walking pace steps of people coming up the stairs speeding into a trampling dash for safety.

"Spotted the bug?" Vikash asked, half to himself.

"Sounds like it. Hold up a sec. We'll run down when the stairs aren't full of screaming mob."

More purposeful voices came from down below — Amanda and Carrington yelling instructions to each other.

"Stay left!"

"I've got it!"

"Don't let her—"

"LJ, drive her back!"

"Fuck!"

"Kyle! Kash!" Carrington finally bellowed. "Coming your way!"

Vikash moved to the left side of the stairs, Kyle to the right. They shook out their nets and gave each other a nod. *Ready.* The sudden skitter of too many chitinous feet on the stairs made Vikash's skin crawl, but he held fast, half-crouched, waiting. Mama Bug burst into the light and Vikash had a split second to think that Jacket wasn't terribly good at describing dimensions. The creature thundering up the stairs might not have been taller than a hot dog cart, but her total mass was closer to a full kitchen food truck.

Head on, they had no chance to stop her. Simple physics. He stepped aside matador-style to allow her to rush past, hoping to get some net on her and slow her down from the side. She had other plans. Abruptly, she veered left and slammed directly into Kyle, knocking him to the sidewalk and fleeing over his prone form. It definitely seemed to be Trample Kyle Underfoot week. Instead of running toward potential open spaces, she took off toward Broad Street.

Of course. "Kyle?"

"I'm fine! Go, damn it! Use those long legs! Right behind you!"

Vikash raced after Mama Bug, her multiple legs moving in a swift glissando, like some hyperspeed alien tank tread. Out of the corner of his eye, he caught the impression of Jacket hurtling up the stairs and stopping to help Kyle up, Carrington and Amanda close behind.

Footsteps pounded behind him. He wasn't alone, but he was out front and had to keep Mama Bug in sight as she dashed down the sidewalk, then made a sharp turn onto Arch Street. She moved improbably fast, crawling over and around traffic. Even at a lung-burning sprint, Vikash struggled to keep up with her. She turned her first few segments, perhaps trying to see how close he was. With a burst of speed, she headed for a set of glass doors.

Vikash's heart gave a hard, anxiety-driven thud. Using her head and mouthparts, she opened the door and wriggled into the building. Mama Bug had decided to try to lose him in the Convention Center. *Decided. Yes.* There was an obvious intelligence working in that tank-like body, not a comforting thought at all.

An immediate flood of people screaming out of the building hampered his pursuit, but he managed to fight upstream in time to get into the lobby before she vanished. Down a nice, wide hallway? No, of course not. She chose to go up the escalator toward the convention area, riding the handrails since her body was too broad for the steps. A ton of people still blocked his way. Some big event was taking place… *Damn*. It was February. The annual auto show was in progress.

He managed to fight through to the escalator just as she gained the top and he leaped up the moving stairs two and three at a time, hoping he hadn't lost his backup in the process. The screaming was getting old. It wasn't as if Mama Bug was stopping to rip people to shreds, though the sight of her coming at a person was unnerving. He skidded to a stop inside the doors to the display area, though it didn't take long to locate her from the flight pattern of high-heeled spokesmodels and manufacturer representatives. Unlike fleeing heroines in certain horror movies though, none of these women in their spikes and pencil skirts fell. They knew how to *move* in those shoes.

Heading through the Ford exhibit, Mama Bug knocked the open door off a truck as she hurried past, heading for the back wall. Weaving through cars and around display walls, Vikash lost her in the strange automotive jungle, catching sight of her briefly as she climbed a wood and steel hill the Jeep folks had set up as a demonstration track. Now she headed for the left side of the floor, toward the Broad Street windows, but by the time Vikash had reached the area, he had lost her and had to stop amid the antique cars, panting.

Footsteps pounded behind him, his colleagues reaching him in various states of breathlessness.

"Where is she?" Kyle gasped out.

Vikash could only shake his head, staring across the street at Lenfest Plaza. He leaned both hands against the railing, trying to pull in a whole breath despite the stitch in his side, and froze.

"Kyle…"

"Aw, man. Seriously?" Kyle made a disgusted sound and headed toward the stairs on this side of the building.

Mama Bug had climbed the Paint Torch and crouched there, King Kong-style, surveying the panic below.

Amanda muttered, "Damn bug."

"She's not a bug, Amanda," Carrington said primly.

"Yeah, well, damn crusty-crab whatever the hell she is." She flipped a hand at him in an irritated way and hurried after Kyle.

"Mr. Jacket." Vikash was surprised that Jacket had kept up the chase. "You and Tim should stay here. This could get ugly."

Leather Jacket held his arms akimbo, as if he were putting his nonexistent hands on his nonexistent hips, while Tim squeaked angrily from his pocket.

"I know, and you've both been incredibly brave. But you're still civilians. I have to ask you to let us do this part."

Jacket made shooing motions with his sleeves, which Vikash took as assent. But as he ran down the stairs and out of the doors, he shot a look over his shoulder. A disembodied black leather jacket floated after him, trying to hide behind a door column as it did so.

Some paranormal entities would do as they pleased. Wasn't much he could do about that. He turned his attention to his fellow officers gathered at the base of the Oldenburg sculpture, where an argument was in progress.

"It's not straight up! I could run up there, easily." Carrington had a hand on the blue paintbrush handle, scowling at his partner.

"The sun's breaking through the clouds," Amanda snapped. "In three minutes, you're gonna get one of your headaches and you'll be fifty feet up when it happens."

"It just really sounds like a bad idea, Carr," Kyle said with his head craned back to keep an eye on Mama Bug.

"It won't take more than a minute. If I can't drag her down, I'll knock her off. When she falls, stunned, we can secure her."

"And when you break your fool vampire neck? What do I tell your new boyfriend?"

Carrington's eyes narrowed as he snarled back, "Nothing. There's no new boyfriend as of last night."

With his net attached to his belt, Carrington ran up the brush handle, despite the piece's sixty-degree angle.

"Damn it, Carr," Amanda said softly, her eyes following his progress. "You didn't even keep that one for forty-eight hours."

As he neared the light-up brush portion of the sculpture, Carrington slowed, approaching the giant pill bug with understandable caution. She managed to curl herself up enough to turn on the absurdly small space to face him, hissing.

"That's not good," Vikash murmured. He edged around the Paint Torch to put himself closer to where the brush combatants would land if they fell, motioning to Kyle to do the same on the other side.

Up top, Carrington was speaking softly, "Easy, easy there, ma'am. You and I, we're both creatures of darkness. I think we can come to an understanding here. No one wants to hurt y — "

She lunged, mouthparts clacking. Carrington ducked to the side to avoid being bitten, lost his balance and in his flailing, managed to snag the leading edge of her third segment. For an agonizing moment, they grappled with each other and gravity. Mama Bug's many legs scrabbled for purchase on the smooth plastic brush, but Carrington's weight proved too much and she slowly slid from her perch. As one being, they fell, Mama Bug curling into an armored pill and Carrington pulling his limbs in close in imitation. They hit the sidewalk with a dull thud, barely missing impalement on the sharp top of the fiberglass paint blob at the bottom of the sculpture.

Both lay terribly still, the whole tableau like the freeze-frame ending of a cheesy eighties movie. Carrington whimpered and the frozen moment shattered as Amanda ran to him while Vikash and Kyle converged on Mama Bug. Vikash had just thrown his net over the rolled-up pill bug and was trying to figure out how to snare her into it more securely, when she suddenly unrolled and took the choice away. His net caught between her segments as she straightened and Vikash could only plant his feet and hang on as she tried to pull away.

"Don't let go!" Kyle called out as he got his net over her head and yanked back, wrapping the end of his net around his fist. "We just have to hold her until we have enough of us to keep her contained!"

Mama Bug would have none of it and lunged forward, yanking both Kyle and Vikash off their feet. Kyle ended up sprawled across her back, Vikash hanging on desperately as she dragged him across the plaza. She slowed and a strange sheen engulfed her, as if a heat shimmer had taken on properties of light. Her form wavered and Vikash got a better grip on the net, anticipating some new escape attempt, when the plaza...vanished.

He still felt the net in his hands, but the world had disappeared. No light, no warmth, no sound. The blackness closed in on him, terrifying and endless. Just when he couldn't hold back a scream any longer, a painful pressure filled his ears and with a pop of displaced air, they were back in the plaza.

They had to hold on. If they lost their grip on her in that blackness, he was sure they would be lost forever. "Net!" Vikash shouted across the bug to Kyle. "Pull it tight!"

In that instant, his heart nearly stopped. He had heard those words, his own words, before, and he lifted his head to meet his own astonished eyes across the plaza. Mama Pill Bug had taken them several hours into the past. In the instant it took him to reach this conclusion, the world vanished again, the blackness stealing breath and sense.

When they popped back into the world again, it was at the correct time, with Carrington waving Amanda off at the end of the plaza and Wolf and Krisk's squad car screeching to a barely controlled stop on Broad Street.

"Kyle! Jump off!" Vikash shouted as Mama Bug shimmered again.

"I can't! My hand's tangled in the damn net!"

Vikash wasn't about to leave him, so he clung fast as she took them back into the dark. When they broke out into the light again, the Convention Center and the Academy of Fine Arts had vanished, replaced by smaller, neat buildings of brick and stone. Horses and mule carts clopped by on the cobblestone road. A woman shrieked and dropped her market basket as they became visible for an instant.

Mama Bug bucked and shook herself, trying to maroon them in colonial Philadelphia. When she couldn't, she shimmered back into the dark and jumped back to the present day plaza where all four of their fellow officers were converging on them. Carrington got close, but the rest weren't fast enough and Mama Bug shimmered back out before anyone reached them.

This time they reemerged in a Philadelphia pre-Europeans, without a person or man-made object in sight. A deer picked up her head, flicking her ears in curiosity, but there were no other witnesses. The peaceful tableau lasted only a single breath before Mama Bug jumped back again.

"Now!" Carrington shouted as they shimmered back into Lenfest Plaza.

Pale, unnaturally strong hands grabbed Vikash by the waist and yanked him off the giant pill bug's back. He landed on top of Carrington, disoriented and winded, where he had a good view of Jacket, wielding a switchblade, cutting the net around Kyle's hand while Wolf got a good grip on Kyle. Before Mama Bug had a chance to try shimmer out again, Krisk barreled into her, knocking her into the wall of the Academy, where she lay on her back with her multitude of feet waving in the air. Stunned, she had ceased to shimmer. Kyle, on hands and knees on the paving bricks, shook his head as if trying to clear water from his ears. The shimmer surrounded *him*, and he popped out of existence.

"Kyle!" Vikash's scream was harsh and raw in his own ears. Carrington still held on to him, keeping him back from the spot where Kyle had vanished.

"Don't enter that space!" Carrington yelled in his ear. "He's done a Kirby and absorbed her abilities. Kyle's teleporting now."

"He's not teleporting. He's time-porting!" Vikash shouted back as he struggled to break free. "I can't lose him. Carr, let go!"

Vikash wrenched free and threw himself across the plaza to where Kyle had been, telling himself that Kyle would reappear in exactly the same spot as Mama Bug had done several times. *Please come back. Please.*

The change in air pressure and the sudden breeze gave him warning. Kyle popped back in, though now he was sprawled on his back, soaking wet. Ocean brine scent rose from him. Something had ripped a jagged hole through his jacket and had bitten into his side. He wasn't breathing.

"No!" Vikash latched on to him. Kyle wasn't getting away again and he wasn't going to *die*, damn it. *Not like this. Not now.* He turned Kyle onto his side, pounding on his back, opening his mouth to see if there was an obstruction. Before he could flip Kyle to his back to start mouth-to-mouth, he was back in the blackness.

They popped out in the peaceful, prehuman meadow of wildflowers. A woolly mammoth grazed quietly nearby.

With trembling hands, Vikash rolled Kyle over and started to breathe for him, keeping a firm hold on his jacket. He'd managed two breaths when they shimmered out again, back to Lenfest Plaza. Kyle was still alive in there if he was still borrowing abilities.

"Kyle! Stop it!" Vikash shouted at him. "How are you doing this unconscious?"

He managed another breath for Kyle before they shimmered out again, this time reappearing in the white and glass city Vikash recognized from his future vision, or visit, or whatever it had been, though Cirrus was nowhere in sight. Kyle began to cough and gurgle. Without losing his grip on Kyle's jacket, Vikash turned him on his side just before they popped out again.

When the light of Lenfest Plaza once again replaced the blackness, Vikash pleaded with a now retching Kyle. "Stop, please. You can do it. Kyle, please. You need help. Can't help if you keep popping back and forth." He gathered Kyle into his arms when he'd finished vomiting primordial seawater, not caring who saw. Another time dislocation to what could have been the late nineteenth century where they were in the middle of the street, and Vikash was growing frantic. A puddle of blood spread under Kyle at each time stop.

"Concentrate, Kyle. Think about where we were. How the plaza looked. Who was there. I think you can hear me. God, I hope so. If we end up doing this forever, I'm with you. Right here. But I'd rather not."

Back to the modern-day plaza.

"I love you," Vikash whispered. "Stay here. Where there's help. Don't die."

Kyle's eyes flickered open. A hint of a smile tugged at his blue lips. "Kash?"

"Right here. Stay here. With me. Please."

"'Kay," Kyle croaked out. "Dizzy. Don't feel good."

Ambulance sirens wailed nearby. Carrington approached cautiously to crouch beside them. "Greg's called in the paramedics. Have you finished your grand tour of time and space?"

"Hope so." Kyle leaned his too-cold face against Vikash's throat. "Not fun."

"Any idea what tried to have you for lunch?" Greg asked as he joined them.

"Ichthyosaurus?" Kyle mumbled. "Big. Scary. All teeth."

The paramedics arrived in a clatter of gurneys and equipment, moving Vikash aside and stripping Kyle out of his ruined jacket. Vikash hovered, terrified that Kyle would vanish again at any moment. For now, his time stream seemed to have stabilized. But something was missing.

"Where's Mama Pill Bug?"

"Gone," Wolf growled from his left. "She popped out while Kyle was having his…whatever that was. Didn't come back."

"It's possible she's decided this period in history is too hazardous for her," Carrington said as he rubbed at his temples. "Perhaps she found more peaceful temporal real estate in which to settle."

"And left all her damn kids behind, I'll bet." Amanda shook her head. "We're gonna be cleaning those little bastards up for weeks."

"More than likely. Amanda?" Carrington's voice began to fade. "It's a bit too sunny out here."

She managed to catch him before he fainted and the paramedics had their hands full with one half-drowned, wounded officer and a sun-stroked vampire. Vikash didn't feel well himself. All the time traveling had made him headachy and nauseous, something they obviously glossed over in *Doctor Who* episodes.

The medics didn't bat an eye when he insisted on riding along to the hospital. Shira promised to take their squad car, along with Jacket and Tim, back to the station, and Wolf said he and Krisk would stay onsite in case Mama Bug decided to return.

* * * *

Several hours, multiple waiting rooms, screenings, radiology and an operating room trip for Kyle later, Vikash sat beside his hospital bed with the last orange rays of daylight painting the room in falsely cheerful tones. At least Kyle wasn't blue any longer. Too pale, but he was breathing well on his own, the broken rib dealt with and the hole in his side patched up. For a few minutes, Vikash simply watched him, unable to banish the anxiety about Kyle vanishing again. So he moved his chair closer and took Kyle's hand, the one not attached to IV lines.

Half an hour went by, then another. Nurses bustled in and out, carefully working around him. No one sneered at the police officer holding his partner's hand. No one said a thing.

When evening had finally darkened from purple to black, Kyle whispered, "Kash?"

"I'm here."

"You're touching me. Someone might see."

"Don't care."

"Oh." Kyle was silent for a few moments. "Can you find me pictures of ichthyosaurs in the morning?"

"Of course."

"Scary critter. Guess I flashed back to when Philly was underwater."

"I'd think so," Vikash agreed softly, squeezing the hand he held. "I'd hate to think there was an airborne ichthyosaurus."

"Ha. Ow. Don't make me laugh. Hurts."

"Sorry. You're done, right?"

"Going all *Quantum Leap*, you mean? How long's it been?"

Vikash had to look at his watch. "Seven…eight hours?"

"Oh, yeah. I'm done. The Kirby effect doesn't last more than a couple hours."

"Good." Vikash rested his head on the mattress beside Kyle's arm, exhaustion settling in. He recalled the words he'd said to Kyle when the terror of losing him was overwhelming. Though he wanted to repeat them, it would be better to wait. Kyle would think he was still overly emotional and didn't mean it. "I'm glad you're here."

"Hey, me too. You just don't know."

* * * *

Three weeks later, Vikash stood in his kitchen, thinking. A purple insulated food carrier sat on the counter, all packed with containers of some of Kyle's favorite vegetarian dishes.

Kyle should be here. The thought was one he'd had several times an hour since Kyle's release from the hospital. But that odd wall was up between them again and Vikash couldn't figure out why. It might have been a stubborn need for independence after being flat on his back in the hospital, but for whatever reason, Kyle had insisted on staying at his own apartment. Vikash stayed with him some nights, but he couldn't sleep in Kyle's too-small bed with him and not hurt him, and Kyle's couch obviously had been transported up from the third circle of spinal hell.

Tonight. The long-put-off conversations had to be tonight. He wasn't sleeping and Kyle, while he was getting better physically, had been snappier and more withdrawn every day.

"I'll be back, Ellie," he said to the inquisitive, fluffy white feline at his feet. When she meowed her assent, he left the food on the counter and grabbed his keys.

It took a few minutes to find a parking spot near Kyle's place just off South Street. On a weeknight, it was challenging. Over the weekend? It approached impossible. He jogged the half block, ran up the stairs and opened the door with the key Kyle had given him.

"Kyle?"

The invalid in question hobbled around the corner into the front foyer. "Hey." Kyle's smile froze, his forehead crinkling. "Didn't you say you were bringing dinner?"

"I, ah, changed my mind." Vikash swallowed hard.

"Okay. I don't think I'm up to eating out."

Vikash waved his hands in negation. "No. Dinner's made. It's just not…here."

Kyle leaned against the wall, scrubbing a hand over his face. "Could you, for once, just spit it out? I'm not gonna scream at you or get out a machete and take your head off, for Christ's sake, Kash. What the hell is going on in that Swiss cheese brain?"

The anger nearly made him change his mind. Kyle was the only person whose anger unnerved him. "I'd like…dinner. It's at my place. We could pack a bag for you? Just…a few days, maybe?"

"Kind of sneaky, don't you think? When I told you no the first time."

Vikash took a step forward, holding his hands back since he wasn't certain his touch would be welcome. "I worry. Am worried. I'll be there more. For you. If you're there." He stopped to pull in a slow breath. "I'm screwing this all up."

"Yeah. I'll say."

Vikash opened Kyle's closet door and pulled out the olive drab duffel as he put his scrambled thoughts back in order. "Please come have dinner at my place. We should talk. We can pack some things for you in case you want to stay."

With an exasperated sound, Kyle shuffled into his living room and lowered himself carefully into the recliner. He looked so tired, so defeated, Vikash thought his heart might crack. "Fine. Whatever you want, Kash. I'm just hungry."

Kyle didn't interfere with the packing and allowed Vikash to pull the car around and to help him down the stairs, which were good things. But the ride over to his apartment was accomplished in stony silence. The reason began to dawn on him. If he guessed right, his social obtuseness was shocking. He knew he had difficulty parsing what other people thought, what their reactions meant, but this was just stupid.

He had to fix it.

As quickly as he could without rushing Kyle up the stairs, he got them inside, installed Kyle on the sofa and set dinner, still warm, on the coffee table. Then he shoved the coffee table out of reach.

"Hey! Starving, injured man here," Kyle protested.

Vikash dropped to his knees in front of Kyle, still keeping his hands to himself. "I won't take long."

Kyle raised an eyebrow. "All right. Let's hear it."

"I'm sorry. For everything. For pushing you away. For not trusting you to keep things polite in public. For making you feel like I was ashamed of you. Because I wasn't. Ever. Ashamed. I just don't do well with public displays—"

Kyle snorted here, but Vikash barreled on, no longer weighing consequences.

"I just don't. And I know you understand the whole work thing. I know you're not stupid. So I'm sorry. That I hurt you. That it's taken me so long. But I don't want to lose you. And I thought I was. Losing you. Then I thought I'd lost you. When you were dead. But you weren't. And I love you. And I want to introduce you to my parents. And hold hands. And go on dates. And I want you to move in with me. Because my apartment's nicer and Ellie likes it here. But if it's too late, if you can't stand the thought because I've been so stupid, I'll still feed you dinner and worry about you."

"So, you did say it." Kyle had his fists clenched on his thighs.

"What?" Vikash fished desperately through his speech. "Which part?"

"The L word. When I was drifting in and out, I swore I heard you say it. You never said it again, though, so I was sure my brain made it up."

"No. I said it." Vikash sat back on his heels, not at all encouraged by Kyle's tone. "I did. My heart was breaking because I was sure I was losing you. Until today, I didn't think about how not saying it again would be…for you. I'm sorry."

Kyle sighed and wrapped an arm around his ribs. "You know that's probably the most I've heard you talk at once since I met you."

"Yes."

"That's better. One word answers. I thought you were broken for a minute."

"No." Vikash lifted his head so he could meet Kyle's weary gaze. "And I do."

"What?"

"Love you."

Kyle held out a hand and waited until he took it before asking, "So, the change of heart was because of a brush with death thing? You think that's sustainable?"

"Yes. No. I mean, yes." Vikash edged closer on his knees and laid his head on Kyle's thigh. "I've loved you all along. But being in law enforcement, it's usually…bad. Really bad. Harassment. Transfers. Someone losing his job."

"You know it's not like that where we are."

"I…know. It took me a while to accept that. Being more open in public, I wasn't sure I could accept. I'm not gay, Kyle."

"I know that. I kinda get where you're coming from. If we're open in public and people see us, they say you are."

The wary tone was back in Kyle's voice. It was time to put an end to all of it and see where it left them. "Yes. It's almost impossible to be openly bi, unless you wear a sign. If I have a girlfriend, I'm supposed to be straight. If I have a boyfriend, I've suddenly come out as gay. Before all the pill bug issues, I felt so guilty that I couldn't give you what you needed. Be what you needed. I was ready to tell you we had to end it so you could find someone better for you."

Kyle made a strangled, wounded sound and Vikash lifted his head.

"Sometimes it takes an awful thing to hit me hard. To sort things out. I don't want to let you go. I don't want you to feel like a dirty secret." Vikash took a breath. Breathing was getting difficult. "As for what people think of us, of me? Fuck them."

That got a shocked laugh from Kyle. "Oh my God! You cussed."

"I did. It's none of their business. So why should I care what conclusions they draw? I want you to move in with me. I want to do better for you."

"Kash," Kyle said it softly, tenderly. "That's a lot to change your mind on. You're worried about me. I get it. When I'm better, you might not feel this way anymore."

"It seems like an abrupt change to you." Vikash tapped his head with one finger. "Because you haven't been in here. I've been processing all this for…a long time."

"Just bet you have." Kyle cupped Vikash's chin, shaking his head from side to side. "I wish you'd talk to me more instead of torturing yourself like this. You know I'll listen."

"It's hard. For me. You know that. To…get thoughts out sometimes."

"More than sometimes." Kyle pulled gently. "Come up here with me. That's better. How about this? I'll keep my place until the lease is up this summer, but I'll live here with you. If we're still both okay with it, then I'll let my place go, okay?"

"Okay." Vikash's heart was pounding for completely different reasons as Kyle rested his head on Vikash's chest and stroked his thigh. "That sounds sensible."

"Good. I've missed you, you big dork." He lifted his head to run his tongue along Vikash's jaw, sending stampedes of ball lightning to his groin. "And I love you, too. I hope you know that."

"Yes." Vikash sucked in a shaky breath. "Kyle?"

"Hmm?"

"I don't want to hurt you."

Kyle sat back to unbutton his shirt. "I know, though I think you mean right now, too. Lemme lie down. We can do a nose to tail thing."

"But—"

"Move now, Soren, or I'm climbing all over you to get into your pants and then I *will* hurt myself."

Vikash snickered at that image. Kyle's eyes left trails of molten light on his skin as he peeled out of his henley and jeans. The socks came off with the jeans, as gracefully as he could manage, then he stopped to help Kyle, who was struggling out of his flannel shirt with obvious difficulty.

"Shh. I have you," Vikash murmured, kissing a soft trail down Kyle's throat to get him to sit still. "Let me take care of you. I know you're tough. Don't need to show me."

"Don't—" Kyle moaned as Vikash slid a hand down his chest. "Coddle."

"Never."

Carefully, Vikash guided his arms out of the sleeves. Kyle had already undone his belt and fly, so it was a simple matter of sliding off the couch with his jeans and briefs. For once, he left everything in an untidy heap on the floor, no folding, no straightening. The dark blush of Kyle's erection lying ready and waiting on his stomach was too much of a temptation, drawing Vikash in irresistibly. Leaning over Kyle's lap, he licked the head just to get one of those beautiful moans from Kyle.

"Killing me, Kash."

"Not what I was going for." Vikash piled the cushions on one end of the sofa, scooted him down that way so his head was supported and helped Kyle swing his legs up.

With Kyle situated, wearing only the wrappings around his healing ribs, Vikash let his gaze roam. Of course he'd seen Kyle naked when he helped him clean up, but this wonderful, decadent sprawl, eyes dark with passion, *this* replaced his heartbeat with thunder.

"So gorgeous, Kash. You don't even know, do you? The way you move, the way you hold yourself, like you don't belong here with the regular humans."

Heat flooded Vikash's face, but he smiled as he slid his boxers off. Careful of where he put his knees and elbows, he prowled up Kyle's body, kissing his way from navel to lips. "If I'm some god's human avatar, someone forgot to tell me. And I want better superpowers, if that's the case."

"You and me both," Kyle muttered as he tangled his fist in the back of Vikash's hair and yanked him down. Their mouths met in a crazed frenzy of lips and tongues, the need built up for weeks breaking free in that moment, a Hoover Dam shattering that swept up every chill and tense moment and sent them screaming downriver.

Vikash let his hands wander gently, relearning Kyle's compact body, shivers racing over his skin as the ridges of Kyle's burn-scarred hands trailed up and down his back. "Can't wait," he panted out against Kyle's shoulder. "Turning around. Don't move."

Without smacking Kyle in the face or elbowing his broken ribs, Vikash turned so his knees straddled Kyle's head. It was a little awkward with one leg jammed into the back of the seat cushions and the other hanging half off the couch, but he didn't care. He cared even less when Kyle's lips closed around the head of his cock, sucking gently.

Nerves whiting out on an overload of pleasure, Vikash rested his head on Kyle's thigh and just let himself feel, rocking his hips and moaning. At some point, he recalled that he really should be doing something. Oh, yes. That lovely cock lay thick and waiting for him on Kyle's stomach. He needed to do something about that.

He licked up the shaft, breathing in Kyle's musk, spice and earth filling his veins, glowing there and warming him from the inside. The neighbors probably heard the moan he got from Kyle when Vikash swallowed him down. Neither one of them would last long. Kyle's sac was already pulling tight and Vikash already felt that electric-pressure that preceded his orgasms. Slow and sensual could come later. This was all about the hunger and Vikash sucked harder, merciless in his pursuit of Kyle's climax.

Only three strokes later, his hands clamped on Kyle's red-furred thighs, he got what he wanted as Kyle cried out around his cock and came in salty, bittersweet jets. Vikash hummed and sucked, wanting every drop, though his humming became desperate moans as Kyle cupped his balls and did that thing with his tongue where it felt like he was everywhere at once.

Dizzy with relief, Vikash let his orgasm wash over him, his blood pounding in his ears because it was Kyle touching him, Kyle stroking him until he shattered. He was still here. The jagged, broken pieces of the world had clicked back into place.

When he could see straight again, he turned carefully, wriggling his way onto the cushions so Kyle could rest against him. It felt so right to have Kyle in his arms again. Nothing had ever felt so right.

"I have conditions, you know," Kyle said on a yawn. "If I move in with you."

"Oh?"

"We're unpacking all those damn boxes in your bedroom."

"But—"

"No arguments. I'm not sleeping in a bedroom where it looks like the owner can't decide if he's gonna stay or not. We're unpacking, finding places to put your shit or giving stuff away if you don't want it. And you're getting your cello out of storage."

"My cello?"

"Yeah. Big string instrument. Usually sits on the floor when played."

"I… My other, ah, lovers always got annoyed when I practiced."

Kyle poked a finger into his chest. "I'm not them. Look, I know you went to college for music. It feels like a part of you that you're hiding from me. I don't want you to hide, to store pieces of you away to avoid arguments. We're getting the damn cello out and I don't care if you don't sound like Yo-Yo Ma at first. You play all you want, the same four notes over and over if you have to."

The ferocity in those last sentences stunned Vikash. He lay there turning over possible answers, because how could one address such fierce love properly? He finally said, "All right. What else?"

"We're allowed to talk about home at work. Nothing inappropriate. But no shushing me if I'm asking about dinner or if we need eggs and stuff."

Vikash nodded at that. It seemed fair if they were sharing an apartment. "Okay. If I shush out of habit, just remind me. And work talk at home?"

"God, yes. I feel like you're trying to shield me right now, not talking about it. Being a cop is stressful enough. Keeping shit bottled up will make you crazy."

"You too, then."

"Seriously, Kash? You know it's harder to get me to *stop* talking."

"But not things that worry you." Vikash pulled the blanket off the back of the couch to cover them and tucked Kyle in closer. "Vance came back to work today."

"Yeah? How's he doing?"

"Not…too bad. He's quiet. Jumpy. Been seeing a therapist. Someone from State Paranormal who won't tell him he imagined things."

"That's good. I hope."

"You don't even like him."

Kyle heaved a slow breath. "I've hated him some days. He can be such a jerk. But I don't wish that kind of thing on anyone and he's still one of ours."

"Hmm. Yes."

"How's Jeff?"

"He's been back for a week. Not working cases. He's helping Jacket and Tim with pill bug recovery. They're working through the city, statue by statue."

"Huh. Well, better him than me. Sounds damn tedious."

"Jeff doesn't mind. Since it's outdoors and mostly peaceful. Tim likes him. Jacket's warmed up to him, too. Lieutenant Dunfee gave Jacket one of the old interrogation rooms. Since we don't use them."

"Like to live in?"

Vikash nodded. "He's been registered an officer-friendly entity at SPU, so he's allowed residence in an official building. Officially. Lieutenant says as long as he keeps his room neat and contraband free, he can stay."

"Well, good. Tim staying with him?"

"Tim has free run of the station. He seems happy."

"By the way, who made the little police hat for him?"

Vikash stifled a snicker. "Ah. Greg. He didn't…make it. It's from a Ken doll he had."

"Oh, man. I *have* to give him shit about that when I get back. What about you?" Kyle nudged him. "I haven't heard a word about what you've been working on."

"Working with Carr and Amanda. Case that looked like one of ours. Turned out to be a human murderer." Vikash shuddered. No, he hadn't wanted to talk to Kyle about that one. The killings had been brutal and sadistic. "Homicide has it now."

"Bad one, huh?" Kyle stroked his side and hugged him tight. "I won't bug you for details. But you know I'm here if it gets bad." He went quiet and Vikash wondered if Kyle had dozed off until he lifted his head. "Hey. What happened to Mama Bug?"

"We're not…sure. We think she ended up in some prehistoric era. Maybe Cretaceous."

"That some weird-ass guess or you have something to base it on?"

Vikash cleared his throat. It had been a shocking and uncomfortable moment. "Vance… Amanda had pictures. Of Mama Bug. He saw them on her screen and, ah, reacted."

"Completely freaked out, huh?"

"Yes. He fell over. Shaking. We thought he was having a seizure. He says he saw her. In his time dislocation."

"I thought he was attacked by pterodactyls."

"Yes. Mama Bug was in the background. Not attacking."

"Got it. Well, okay. I hope she's doing all right there and I'm kinda hoping she stays there. Then. You know what I mean."

"I do." Vikash turned his head to kiss the shock of uncombed red hair beneath his chin. Kyle had been letting it go while he was on leave and while Vikash liked it longer, it was probably time to encourage a visit to the barbershop. "Your food is getting cold."

Kyle nestled closer, burrowing under the blanket. "Lemme rest here just a sec. Don't mind if it's not hot. Your food's good enough to eat cold."

"Is it?"

"Hell yeah. Why do you think I always beg leftovers from you? I eat them cold for breakfast."

Vikash swatted his hip and an odd sound escaped him, shocking in its volume. It was a laugh. Something he didn't recall uttering since he'd been small. The only explanation lay beside him. Kyle could do that to him, surprise a smile from him, or even a laugh. Kyle filled that empty space that had dogged his steps for years, understood without effort, insisted on having all of Vikash, even the neurotic spots. How had he ever thought he could give this up and just go on with life?

"I hated you the first time I saw you," Kyle said softly. "Or I tried to. You were so perfect, so confident, and gorgeous. And tall."

"I'm sorry."

"Ha. Yeah. Not your fault. Wanna know how long I managed to hate you?"

"Maybe?"

"Didn't even last through that first ride together to the morgue. Your weird matched up with my weird too well. I felt like I'd found someone I'd lost. Like you'd been waiting out there for me to find you again."

"I suppose I have been. Was. Waiting for you."

"So you're ready to meet my mom this weekend, right?"

A thin thread of panic wound around Vikash's heart. "*This* weekend?"

Kyle set up far enough to face him. "Yeah, why? You have big plans or something?"

Vikash shook his head, trying to yank the rising social terror down and stamp it underfoot.

"That's what I thought." Kyle's eyes narrowed. "It's either this weekend or you come for Easter dinner when the whole clan's there. Brothers, wives, rugrats and all. Your choice."

"Ah. So we're resorting to emotional blackmail?"

"Part of any good relationship."

Vikash combed his fingers through Kyle's hair and waited for him to nestle back against his shoulder. "All right. This weekend. I…I do want to meet your mom." As he said it, he found he really did, awkward social panic aside. He wanted to meet Kyle's family, the whole, boisterous extended tribe to understand the people who had made Kyle into Kyle. "This is going to work, isn't it?"

"It better." Kyle sat up again, finally surveying the food laid out on the coffee table. "I like your apartment so much better than mine."

A smaller, comfortable laugh got away from Vikash. As he reached for a plate and piled a little of everything on it for Kyle, he found he didn't mind the laugh. With Kyle, he would never have to hide or keep such tight control over everything. Safe. Happy. Loved. This was what it was like finally to be home.

About the Author

The unlikely black sheep of an ivory tower intellectual family, Angel Martinez has managed to make her way through life reasonably unscathed. Despite a wildly misspent youth, she snagged a degree in English Lit, married once and did it right the first time, (same husband for almost twenty-four years) gave birth to one amazing son, (now in college) and realized at some point that she could get paid for writing.

Published since 2006, Angel's cynical heart cloaks a desperate romantic. You'll find drama and humor given equal weight in her writing and don't expect sad endings. Life is sad enough.

She currently lives in Delaware in a drinking town with a college problem and writes Science Fiction and Fantasy centered around gay heroes.

Angel loves to hear from readers. You can find their contact information, website details and author profile page at http://www.pride-publishing.com.